A Ponderosa Resort
Romantic Comedy

Hottie Lumberjack

USA Today Bestselling Author

TAWNA FENSKE

HOTTIE LUMBERJACK

A PONDEROSA RESORT ROMANTIC COMEDY

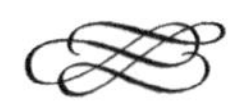

TAWNA FENSKE

This is a work of fiction. Names, characters, organizations, places, events, and incidents are either products of the author's imagination or are used fictitiously.

www.tawnafenske.com

Cover design by Craig Zagurski

ABOUT HOTTIE LUMBERJACK

When Mark Bracelyn lumbers into Chelsea Singer's cupcake shop with an axe, she's poised to hit the panic button. But he fixes her door, praises her buttercream, and sends her skittish heart pounding like a hammer on a hollow log, so he can't be all that scary. Chelsea's sure there's a gooey marshmallow center under Mark's tough outer shell, though admittedly she's been wrong before.

Mark may look like a grungy lumberjack, but he's also the wealthy part-owner of Ponderosa Luxury Ranch Resort. The lone Bracelyn heir to avoid a childhood of fancy boarding schools, he stays hidden behind the scruffy beard and battered truck. But something else separates Mark from his siblings, and keeping his guard up means keeping his secret—and his family.

When someone threatens Chelsea and her daughter, Mark becomes their personal protector. When he's not watching her back, he's watching the rest of Chelsea's body and warning himself not to touch. With danger mounting, they bond over phallic cupcakes and bizarre bunny behavior, while Mark battles his surging attraction. Can a sweet-toothed mountain man and a cautious single mom escape their histories, or will their hearts land on the chopping block?

ALSO IN THE PONDEROSA RESORT ROMANTIC COMEDY SERIES

- Studmuffin Santa
- Chef Sugarlips
- Sergeant Sexypants
- Hottie Lumberjack
- Stiff Suit
- Mancandy Crush (novella)
- Captain Dreamboat
- Snowbound Squeeze (novella)
- Dr. Hot Stuff (coming soon!)

To Cedar and Violet,
For being my daily reminder that
family requires no shared DNA.

CHAPTER 1

CHELSEA

"Here you go, Mrs. Sampson." I slide the pink bakery box across the counter with a smile. "One dozen Guinness chocolate cupcakes with chai spice frosting, and one dozen strawberry with vanilla fondant."

My retired math teacher pulls the box to her chest like she thinks someone will snatch it. "Did you put the penises on top like I asked?"

Her volume is a good indication she forgot her hearing aid, and the chime of my front door is a good indication of how my week's going. I order myself to stay focused on the customer in front of me, but from the corner of my eye I see the new arrival flinch in surprise.

"I'll be with you in just a—*oh*."

Holy shit.

The guy in the doorway of my bakery doesn't look like someone shopping for a dozen vanilla bean cupcakes. He looks like a lumberjack who lost his way to the forest. The scruffy beard, the plaid flannel, and ohmygod is that an *axe*?

I swallow hard and glance at Mrs. Sampson, reminding myself not to alarm her. If we're going to die at the hands of an axe murderer, I'd like her to go out knowing she got what she wanted in that bakery box. "The cupcakes are made to order, just like always," I assure her. "I even slipped in a couple complimentary macarons because I know Mr. Sampson loves them."

She frowns but doesn't turn around to notice the hulking figure behind her. "But the penises," she says. "They're for a bachelorette party for my grand-niece and—"

"You've got your penises." I wince at the sharpness of my words, wishing desperately we could stop saying that word in front of a guy who presumably has one. I'm trying not to look. "And I've got your order for next week's Welfare Society luncheon. Can I get you anything else, Mrs. Sampson?"

"No, dear," she says, finally convinced that I successfully piped one dozen flesh-colored phalluses onto her pastries. "You're a doll, Chelsea. I hope you find a man soon."

As if that weren't embarrassing enough, she reaches across the counter and pats my cheek. Then she turns and brushes past the man who's looking more than a little regretful about walking in here.

I get a better look at him this time, and nope, I didn't imagine the axe. Or the fact that he has to be at least six-five, which means he has to duck to get under the doorframe as he holds it open for Mrs. Sampson.

"Ma'am." His voice is gruff, but his eyes are kind. "You need help getting that into your car?"

"Thank you, Mark," she says. "I've got it. You tell that sister of yours hello."

"Yes, ma'am."

Sister? Mark?

I study the guy more closely but see zero resemblance to five-foot-nothing Bree Bracelyn, the marketing VP for Ponderosa Ranch Luxury Resort. But this has to be the brother she's talked about for months, right?

The door swings shut and Paul Bunyan—er, Mark—turns to

face me. He scrubs a hand over his beard as he ambles toward the counter. "I need cupcakes."

I glance at the axe in his hand and nod. "Uh, you're in the right place for that."

Folding my hands on the counter, I meet his eyes. They're a warm brown like my favorite Guittard chocolate, and I forget for a moment that he could crush my skull with his hands if he wanted to. He doesn't appear to want to, but I don't have a history of being a great judge of men.

I push aside dark thoughts about my daughter's sperm donor and the half-dozen other men in my past who've turned out to be real doozies and focus on the more immediate threat. Or is there a threat? Hottie Lumberjack doesn't look terribly menacing. There's an odd sort of teddy bear quality to the guy, if teddy bears had massive biceps and broad shoulders and sharp pieces of weaponry in their paws.

He catches me staring and sets the axe down beside my display case, leaning it against his thigh. That's huge, too. Everything about this guy is enormous, so why do I feel more turned on than terrified?

The guy clears his throat. "I'm supposed to order two dozen cupcakes for a bunch of tour operators from—"

"I'm sorry, why do you have the axe?"

He cocks his head, genuinely perplexed. "For chopping wood."

For fuck's sake. "I mean why did you bring it into a cupcake shop?"

I'm no longer worried he's here to lop my head off, but still.

He stares at me for a few beats, not answering, not blinking, not even smiling. Not that I could tell, what with the thick beard masking any sort of expression. But I can see his lips, which are full and soft and—

"Sharp."

I blink. "What?"

"The axe," he says. "Had to get it sharpened."

"So you brought it to a cupcake shop?"

The corners of his mouth twitch, but he doesn't smile. "No, I brought it to the shop down the street. Didn't want to leave it in the truck because the doors don't lock. Safety hazard."

"Oh." That actually makes sense.

Sort of. If this is really Bree Bracelyn's brother, he's a freakin' gazillionaire. Not that any of the siblings in that family act like it, but it's common knowledge the Bracelyn kids inherited a lot more than their dad's ranch when he died.

Suffice it to say, Hottie Lumberjack could afford a truck that locks.

"Chelsea Singer," I tell him, wiping a hand on my pink and green striped apron before offering it to him. "I own Dew Drop Cupcakes." As an afterthought, I add, "And I'm not an axe murderer."

His mouth definitely twitches this time. "Mark Bracelyn. Ponderosa Resort. Also not an axe murderer."

"Good. That's good." And interesting. He didn't volunteer his job title, but I know it's something like Vice President of Grounds Management, which Bree told me he *hates*. He might be part-owner of a luxury resort for rich people, but he'd rather be regarded as the handyman. That's what Bree says, anyway.

And don't think I haven't noticed Bree filling my head with Mark-related tidbits.

Mark built me a new woodshed this weekend.

Mark has a major sweet tooth.

Mark rescued a family of orphaned bunnies yesterday.

I'm not sure whether she wants me to date him or just think twice about macing him if we meet in a dark alley, but it's odd this is the first time we're meeting.

"So Mark," I say, leaning against the counter. "What can I get for you?"

"Cupcakes." He frowns. "Two dozen."

"Right, but any particular flavor? Strawberry, peanut butter, kiwi, red velvet, double-fudge—" I stop when I see the dazed look in his eyes and nudge a laminated menu across the counter at him. "We have more than fifty cake flavors and three dozen frosting varieties, plus fondant and icing. There's an infinite variety of combinations."

Those brown eyes take on the ultimate "kid in a candy shop" glow, so I give him a private moment while I turn and wash my hands at the sink. His eyes become saucers as I turn back and reach into the display case to pull out a tray of mini cupcakes. I wouldn't do this for every customer, but Ponderosa Resort is one of my biggest clients.

"This is one of our seasonal favorites right now," I explain as I pluck a soft baby cupcake off the tray. "It's Guinness chocolate, and it's great with the Irish cream frosting. Would you like to try it?"

"Yes." His throat moves as he swallows. "Yes, please."

The gruff eagerness in his voice makes my girl parts clench, which is ridiculous. And a sign of how long it's been since I had sex, which....um, yeah. Let's just say dating's not easy for single moms.

I whip out a pastry bag and do a quick swirl of frosting on top of the cupcake. "Here you go."

Our fingers touch as I hand it across the counter, and I suppress an involuntary shiver. The good kind of shiver, like the one I do every time I bite into a perfect snickerdoodle. Good Lord, this guy has massive hands. He makes my mini cupcake look like a chocolate chip. "See what you think of that."

I have to look away from the expression of rapture on his face. There's something raw and intimate about it, and my belly's doing silly somersaults under my apron. I survey my tray, trying to come up with another good flavor combo.

"Let's see, this is one of Bree's favorites." I steal a look at his face, but if he's surprised I connected the dots to his sister, he doesn't show it. He's too fixated on his cupcake, savoring every little mini-bite like it's an act of worship.

This shouldn't be getting me hot, right?

I clear my throat and swirl some lime zest frosting onto a lemon cupcake. "Bree likes the citrus combo," I tell him. "Is it a family thing?"

Something odd flashes in his eyes, but he takes the mini cupcake and nods. "Thank you."

He eats this one more gingerly, still savoring every crumb. I glance down at the sample tray and try to think of what other flavors to offer. What would a guy like Mark Bracelyn enjoy? I don't make manly-man confections like sawdust cupcakes with drizzles of pine sap or mini-cakes infused with hints of leather and charcoal briquette. But maybe something on the other end of the spectrum.

"These tend to be too sweet for some people, but—"

"Yes." He nods. "Yes, please, I'd like to try it."

I smile and pluck a gooey-looking confection off the edge of the tray. "You're in luck, I had some left over from a kids' birthday party order. This is my coconut caramel chocolate delight cupcake. It's like those Girl Scout cookies—Samoas?—but in cupcake form."

The sheer joy in this man's eyes is enough to make my hand shake as I place it in the center of his massive palm. He lifts it to his mouth, and I swear on my KitchenAid mixer, I have a mini-orgasm. If the way to a man's heart is through his stomach, the way into my pants is through a man's sweet tooth.

What? No, I didn't just think that.

Holy shit, Chelsea, get it together.

I smooth out my apron as Mr. Tall, Gruff, and Silent polishes off his cupcake. I consider offering him more—cupcakes, not sexual favors—but what's that expression about free milk and cow buying and—

Great, now I'm thinking about Mark Bracelyn's hands on a pair of udders, which sooooo shouldn't be hot, but it is.

Stop it.

I clear my throat. "So what'll it be?" I ask. "You didn't mention when you need the order, but I have several of these in stock. Most will take a couple days, though."

Mark wipes his beard with a sleeve, and I realize I should have offered a napkin. He doesn't seem to need one, though, and his beard is remarkably crumb-free. What's it like to kiss a guy with facial hair? I've only experienced five-o-clock shadow, the sort of sandpaper scruff that leaves your cheeks raw and red. But Mark's beard looks soft, with hints of cinnamon and nutmeg.

Stop thinking of this man as edible.

"I'll take four dozen, please," he says.

I bite my lip, not positive I've got that much stock. "I thought Bree only needed two dozen."

"She does," he says. "The extras are for me. A dozen of whatever you've got in stock now, and the rest can wait 'til Friday."

I smile and jot the order on a notepad. "Got it. You want anything specific, or a mixed batch?"

He doesn't smile, but there's a flicker of interest in his eyes. "Surprise me."

Oh, baby.

"How about any pupcakes?" I offer.

Mark frowns. "Pupcakes?"

"Cupcakes for dogs," I say. For some reason I just assumed he has a dog. He looks like the sort of guy who'd have a Rottweiler or maybe a blue ox named Babe. "Bree buys them all the time for Virginia Woof."

"I should get a dog." He says this with an earnestness that makes my heart go gooey.

"You totally should." Good Lord, why am I advising this man on his life choices? "The Humane Society has tons of great ones. My daughter and I volunteer there every Saturday."

This is where most guys check out. Or check my ring finger. Or ask some not-so-subtle question about the baby-daddy, even though everyone pretends not to care. Plenty of folks have heard rumors.

But Mark doesn't blink. Just looks me in the eye, calm and steady. "Good idea."

"Which? Volunteering at the Humane Society, or you getting a dog."

"Yes."

I wait for more, but there doesn't seem to be any. His attention shifts to something over my shoulder, and he points one enormous finger. "How long's that been like that?"

I look where he's pointing and see the banged-up handle on the side door leading to the alley. I left it open a few inches to let the spring breeze waft through, and it's obvious even from here that someone messed with the doorknob.

"A couple days." I turn back to face him. "I came in the other morning and found it like that. Probably kids messing around. I haven't had time to call the repair guy."

Mark frowns. "May I?"

I'm not sure what he's asking, but I nod like an idiot. "Sure."

He lumbers around the counter, leaving his axe behind. After a few seconds of fiddling with the lock and muttering, he marches back around the counter. "Wait here."

"I—"

The front door swings shut behind him before I can point out that I've got no place to go, owning the shop and everything. He's not gone more than a minute, and when he strides back through the door, he's carrying a battered red toolbox.

He doesn't ask this time. Just rounds the corner and goes to the door again. There's some hammering and rattling, a few curse words that make me glad it's a slow weekday and there are no other customers around. I busy myself filling a bakery box with cupcakes, slipping in two extras and one of my cupcake-shaped business cards with a few words scrawled on the back.

Then I wander toward the door, watching his shoulders bunch as he works. He's rolled up the sleeves of his flannel shirt, revealing forearms thick and ropey with muscle. The man is huge, even kneeling on my floor.

I don't realize how close I've crept until he turns his head and—

"Um," he says.

He's face-to-boob with me, and we're frozen in the moment. I could step forward and feel the tickle of his beard against my breasts through the front of my T-shirt. He could lean in and whisper warm breath against my nipples, making them pucker through the lace of my bra.

But neither of us does that.

He's first to lift his gaze, meeting my eyes through a haze that looks like the same thing buzzing through my brain. "You're good."

"What?"

"The door." He gestures with a screwdriver but doesn't break eye contact. "That should hold now. No need to call a repairman."

I drag my eyes from his and see he's fixed my damn door. How about that?

"Wow." I step back at last, aware of the dizzy hum pulsing through my core. "That's—wow. What do I owe you?"

Mark stands and hoists his toolbox, wiping a hand on his jeans. "You gave me cupcake samples."

"Maybe a dollar's worth of samples," I point out. "A repairman would charge at least a hundred."

"You can give me a pupcake," he says. "When I get my dog."

He gives me a small smile, but I don't think he's kidding. I do think he's considering kissing me. I want him to, Jesus God, I want him to, and it's the craziest thing ever.

But he turns and lumbers back around the counter. Setting

down the toolbox, he fishes into his pocket and comes up with a battered leather wallet. "For the four-dozen cupcakes," he says, laying four hundred-dollar bills on the counter as my jaw falls open.

How much does this man think I charge for butter and sugar and—

"It was good meeting you." He gathers his axe and toolbox and the pink bakery box, then lumbers toward the door before I can muster any words like "wait" or "your receipt" or "please bend me over the counter."

The door swings shut behind him, and seconds later, a truck engine growls to life. I realize my mouth is still hanging open, so I close it and watch a faded blue and white pickup rumble down the street.

What the hell just happened?

CHAPTER 2

MARK

My plan to avoid sibling contact until I've calmed the fuck down lasts roughly nineteen seconds after I get home from meeting the woman of my goddamn dreams.

That's Chelsea, in case it wasn't obvious.

And that's Bree, my pain-in-the-ass sister, banging on the door of my cabin just as I've dropped into an oversized leather chair and popped open a can of grape soda.

"What?" I ask, soda can gripped in one hand.

I've cracked the door only a few inches, but my sister shoves her way inside like a curly-haired bulldog and marches right past me. Even in her high-heeled shoes, she barely comes up to the middle of my ribcage.

"We have a meeting," she announces, grabbing the soda can from my hand and taking a slug. She makes a face. "How can you drink this stuff? It's pure sugar."

I snatch the can back. "What meeting?"

She rolls her eyes. "The pre-meeting for tomorrow's meeting of the entire resort ownership team. Remember? Jonathan is flying in?"

Crap. She's right; all four of us who live on-site—me, Bree, Sean, and James—plus our brother Jonathan, who's been halfway around the globe doing God knows what with some humanitarian group, we're set to have some sort of annual review. It's the first time in ages that the core of Bracelyn sibs will be under one roof, and Bree's been talking about it for weeks.

An uneasiness settles in my belly as I think about sitting down with all those pedigreed half-sibs with their dark hair and eerie green eyes.

"Who the fuck has pre-meetings?" I ask. "Isn't one meeting enough?"

More than enough, actually. I love my brothers and sister, but holy hell, what is it with them and meetings?

Bree sighs, but she's not really annoyed. She's only here to quiz me about Chelsea anyway, but I might as well make her work for it.

She leans against the wall and grabs my soda again. "Jonathan hasn't been here since before we opened." She takes another slug of soda and makes a face. "Hell, James is the only one who's seen him recently, and that was just to sign all the legal paperwork saying we could run his share of the resort however we want."

I consider opening a can of soda just for her, but I'd rather not prolong this discussion. I'm not a fan of conversations about the awkward family dynamic. All of us—Bree, Sean, Jon, James, and God knows how many other Bracelyn progeny are out there running around—have different mothers, and most of us grew up in different states. I was raised right here in Oregon, the only kid to somehow avoid getting hauled off to some snobby boarding school.

That's not the only thing that separates me from the rest of the bastard Bracelyn clan, but I digress.

"Come on, Mark," she says. "You're part of this family and a member of the leadership team. We need you."

Something knots up tight in my gut, and it's not because I'm needed. That's the part I like, the part that leaves me feeling like I have a place in this whole crazy plan to turn Dad's ranch into a luxury resort.

You're part of this family.

I grab the soda can and gulp until I don't hear Bree's words anymore. "I'll be there in five."

"Great." She grins and leans back against the wall. "So, how was she?"

Gotta appreciate that my sister's not even pretending there wasn't an ulterior motive behind her cupcake errand. She's been on me for months to meet the owner of the cupcake shop. Blame my sweet tooth for the fact that I caved.

"She's nice."

Nice.

Bree's not the only one who knows what a bullshit answer that is. *Nice* is for tepid water and saltine crackers. Not for stunning brunettes with fiery streaks in her hair and clear blue eyes and freckles like sprinkles of cocoa powder on her nose. God, those eyes. And that mouth. And—

"Hello? Earth to Mark." Bree frowns. "You did remember to order the cupcakes, right?"

"Yeah." I clear my throat. "She'll have them ready for you to grab on Friday."

"Oh." My sister frowns. "You're not picking them up for me?"

There. That's my opening. My chance to see Chelsea again.

But no, that's a bad idea. Like a bull in a china shop—or a toddler in a cupcake shop—I'll just make a mess of things. Besides, she's got a kid. I know damn well how messed up it is for a kid to bounce between his dad and his mom's "man friends" with no real certainty who's staying or going and who the hell that makes you in the grand scheme of things.

I might have issues, as Bree would say.

"Come on," I tell her now. "Let's go to the pre-meeting."

She watches my face for a moment, then grabs back my soda can and polishes it off. When she sets the empty can on my counter, determination glints in her eyes. "We're not done here."

I close my eyes and sigh, pretty sure she's right.

* * *

IT'S NEARLY eight-thirty by the time I make it back to my cabin.

It's both a blessing and a curse having a brother who's a Michelin-starred chef. A curse, because every meeting turns into a three-hour, six-course dinner party.

A blessing because it's fucking delicious.

And because I love my family. I do, even though I don't always show it. Even though I'm not sure I belong.

I kick my boots off by the door and head for the fridge. I shouldn't still be hungry, but it takes a lot of calories to fuel someone my size. Besides, I haven't stopped thinking about those cupcakes all night.

Fine. *Fine,* it's Chelsea I haven't stopped thinking about, but I'll take the cupcakes if I can't have her.

You can have her. You caught the vibes coming off of her back there.

It's not a matter of interest. I'm not stupid; I can tell when a woman's into me. True, her interest has a sweet, warm quality, while mine might trend more toward nuclear energy. Either way, the chemistry's there.

But no. That's a dangerous path to start down, the single mom thing. I could pick up the phone right now and call my own mom if I wanted a reminder of that.

Mistress to a millionaire—okay, gazillionaire—my mom bore zero resemblance to Cort Bracelyn's other wives. That's probably why she never became one, content to turn down his marriage proposals while raising me mostly on her own.

I've wondered sometimes if that's what kept him hanging

around. The fact that my mother left him wanting, that he stuck around waiting for her to say yes—is that what made me the only Bracelyn kid who got dear ol' dad in his life on the regular?

Or maybe it was proximity, the fact that he liked coming out to his vanity ranch in Oregon. Maybe that's why he sometimes did normal dad stuff like showing up for Little League games and even the occasional dinner while my brothers and sister got fat checks and tiny scraps of time during their boarding school breaks.

Shaking off the grim thoughts, I open the bakery box and pull out three cupcakes. One with pale yellow frosting that I fear might be lemon—not my favorite—but that turns out to be pineapple. That, and something chocolate, plus another with pink frosting and a fresh raspberry in the center. I slide them all onto a plate and start to close the lid when I notice the card.

At first I think it's just a business card—one shaped like a cupcake, but a business card nonetheless. Then I spot handwriting on the back.

Mark,

Would love to hear how you like the caramelized pineapple, it's a new flavor.

That's followed by a tiny heart and her name. Below that is a phone number. I flip the card to see the digits are different from the ones on the front, which means she's given me her personal number.

Don't do it. Don't call. Don't fuck this up.

But I'm already dialing.

She picks up on the second ring sounding breathless and cheerful. "Hello?"

I hesitate. I could hang up now, pretend it was a wrong number or something.

But my big, dumb heart forces the words into my throat without consulting the rest of me.

"Chelsea," I say. "It's Mark. Mark Bracelyn."

CHAPTER 3

CHELSEA

I'm not sure what stuns me more—that I had the guts to scribble my phone number on that note to Mark, or that he actually dialed it.

He's silent on the other end of the line, but I can hear him breathing. Can picture him sitting on a sofa with his big arms spread across the back and a plate of cupcakes on his knee.

"Mark," I say when I find my voice. "It's great to hear from you. Did you like the caramelized pineapple?"

"I'm eating it now." His voice is a low rumble, and I swear this is my equivalent of phone sex. Sitting here, knowing a man I'm hot for is devouring something I baked.

"And?" I hate how breathless I sound, how needy. This isn't like me.

"It's great. I didn't expect that."

"To like my cupcakes?" I'm not flirting, I swear. Just looking for honest feedback.

"Caramel and pineapple," he says. "I wouldn't put those things together, but it's good."

I curl my feet up under me on the sofa, grateful Libby has already turned in for the night. In a few months when she's seven, she'll probably start pushing back on the eight-thirty bedtime. For now, it's a blessed relief to have some quiet time to myself at the end of a long day.

"I love playing with unique flavor combinations," I tell him. "Things you wouldn't think go together sometimes do."

He's silent for a long time, and I wonder if I pushed my luck. If he heard that as a come-on, or if I'm blathering on with stuff his famous chef brother has already told him.

When he speaks, his voice is low and rich as molasses. "Like chocolate and peanut butter."

"Sure, or you know what's even better?"

"What?"

"Chocolate and sesame." I'm being a food geek, but I don't care. I could talk about this stuff all night. I snuggle back on my couch, wondering what it's like to cuddle with a guy as big as Mark. Would that beard tickle the back of my neck? Would arms that size feel comforting wrapped around my middle, or like a pair of anacondas poised to crush the life out of me?

Something tells me it's the former.

Food. Right, we're talking about food. "Sesame has a more complex, savory flavor than peanut," I tell him. "Mixing it with chocolate is decadent, especially if you throw in a little Himalayan pink sea salt."

"Wow. That's—you're getting me all worked up."

Oh, Jesus.

He didn't mean that in a sexy way, *he didn't.*

But my body responds like he's whispering dirty words in my ear. I keep going, hungry for more of that same response.

"You know what else is great with chocolate?"

"What?"

I lick my lips, part of me wanting to blurt out a desire to drizzle it on my breasts and have him lick it off.

Down, girl.

"Avocado," I tell him. "It adds this creamy, silky texture, and this amazing richness. I do a mousse sometimes that's great on my red velvet cake."

"God."

I'm not imagining it. He sounds as turned on as I feel. I keep going, totally in my element. "Spice is good, too," I tell him. "With chocolate. I do a raspberry jalapeno cupcake with bittersweet chocolate that's really popular around the holidays, and a flourless chocolate cayenne cake that's to-die-for with—"

"Stop. Chelsea, you're killing me."

His protest is gruff and breathless, and I look down to discover my fingertips skimming my nipple through the thin cami top I'm wearing. I draw my hand back fast, thankful my daughter is a sound sleeper. What the hell am I doing?

I clear my throat and try to think of something non-food porny to talk about. "So you're the handyman." I glance down at my hand grazing the junction of my thighs and shift it to my knee fast. "At the resort," I clarify. "And with my door. Thanks again for—"

"Yeah," he says. "I've always been good at fixing stuff."

I wait, wondering if he'll say more. Tell me about building things with his dad or splitting wood for his sister. When the silence stretches for more than a few heartbeats, I hustle to fill it.

"Did you learn that from your dad, or—"

"Yeah."

One syllable. I can't even tell from the tone if it's a happy one or bittersweet. His father died a couple years ago, and though I never met him, his financial status was legendary. "I'm sorry he passed," I murmur. "He must have been a great guy."

"Sometimes."

Another one-word answer. Another long stretch of me waiting to hear if there's more or if that's pretty much it.

Mark clears his throat, and I grip the phone tighter. "Kinda weird for a wealthy guy with mansions all over the world to be handy with tools," he says. "But he was."

There's definite nostalgia in his voice, and I suspect I've just gotten a rare glimpse into the inner workings of Mark Bracelyn. I hold my breath, waiting for more.

I wait a long time.

Finally, I can't take the silence. "Bree says you built most of the cabins at the resort," I say. "You and your cousin, Brandon."

"We all did," he says gruffly, not clarifying who "we" might be, but clearly not loving the spotlight shining too brightly on him as a solo act. "Sean and James and I did the tables in the restaurant."

"Sean is the chef and James is the—"

"Boss man. Lawyer. Yep."

"Wow." I'm even more impressed than I was a few minutes ago. I've seen those tables, and assumed they came from some overpriced boutique. "You're talented."

"Thanks."

I want to ask more. About his dad and his mom and his childhood and how he ended up becoming the guy he is now.

But something tells me not to push. Mark Bracelyn's like a soufflé. Rush it or jack up the temperature or bang the pan too hard and the whole thing collapses. But if you're patient and gentle and—

"How about you?" he asks.

"Me?"

"How'd you learn to bake?"

"Oh. My grandmother. She owned a bakery in Portland. A famous one, near the Pearl District."

"Portland," he says. "My mom's got a place there."

"Do you visit much?"

"As often as I can."

"So, you're close."

"Yes." One word, crisp and cautious, is enough to tell me I'm treading closer to something he doesn't want to discuss.

But he surprises me. "My mom's the best," he says. "Not perfect—not by a fucking long shot—but kind and smart and funny and doesn't take shit from anyone. *Anyone.* She's the best person I know."

Wow.

I have trouble finding my voice. "You know, it's every mother's dream to have a kid who talks about her like that," I say. "I hope my daughter does that with me someday."

"What's her name?"

"Libby. Short for Elizabeth, but she's really more of a Libby."

"Libby," he repeats, and there's something unbearably sweet about hearing my daughter's name spoken in Mark's gruff voice. "That's pretty."

"Thank you. She's named after—"

Bing-bong.

"Dammit." I scramble off the couch, hoping whoever the hell is ringing the bell at this hour doesn't wake Lib. "Hang on a sec."

"You expecting company?"

"No." I peer through the window beside the door, but there's no one out there. I flip on the light and scan the sidewalk. No one. "It's been happening a lot. Just neighborhood kids playing ding-dong-ditch, I guess."

"Huh." Mark's quiet for a second. "You keep your doors locked?"

"Um, mostly?" I laugh, but it's an uneasy laugh. "I should probably be better about it. I grew up here when there were like thirty-thousand people, and no one ever locked their doors. It's a hard habit to get into now that the population's tripled."

He doesn't say anything right away, and I feel dumb. "I'll do better," I tell him.

"I want you to stay safe." There's something soft and comforting in his voice, and I'm not sure we're talking about my security habits.

"I am," I assure him. "I'm a big girl, Mark. I've been taking care of myself for a long time."

He gives a muffled grunt, and I flip the lock on my front door and throw the deadbolt. "I should probably go."

I don't want to. I want to stay up all night talking with Mark about cupcakes and food porn and families.

"Yeah," he says. "Probably smart."

But neither of us hangs up, which probably proves my mother was right about me having the world's worst judgment.

Right now, I don't care. Right now, I want to snuggle back on the couch and tell Mark a bedtime story about Grandma's monster cookies and the red vinyl stool she'd let me stand on to stir the mixing bowls.

And so I do.

CHAPTER 4

MARK

I know it was dumb to stay up 'til midnight talking on the phone with Chelsea. Dumb, not just because I swore I'd keep my distance, but because I'm fighting like hell to stay awake in this meeting.

Not that this is new.

"If you'll all turn to page sixteen in the business plan…"

James is in full-on CEO mode, but I do what he says, grateful he's in charge and not me. When we divvied up our roles at the start of this whole crazy resort project, everyone had a place. Bree's got the fancy marketing degree and Sean's a world-famous chef, so it was clear where they belonged. James, with his law degree and business sense, was a good fit to be in charge, plus no one else wanted to do it.

And then there was me.

I'm good with my hands and have a general contractor's license and the know-how to do everything from electrical work to framing to golf course irrigation. It's what I'm happy doing, but it doesn't take a rocket scientist to notice that—in the words of that old Sesame Street jingle—*one of these things is not like the other.*

I glance around the table at all those matching green eyes and business-mode postures and wonder if they've ever noticed.

"What do you think, Mark?" James studies me over the top of his sheaf of papers. I stare back, wondering what the hell he's just asked.

"Uh—"

"Mark and I actually met last week to discuss this." Bree smiles as she throws me a rope. "If he can get those last two cabins built by end of summer, I've got a reporter from *Sunset Magazine* who's dying to write about them."

I telegraph my gratitude to Bree as James flips another page. "And you think that's doable, Mark?"

"Yeah."

My brother waits only half a breath before forging ahead with the meeting. None of us exactly grew up together, but everyone's gotten used to each other's quirks. Mine are many, but mostly the fact that I don't feel the need to spew a hundred words when one or two will do just fine.

As James keeps talking about Q4 goals and benchmarks, I survey my brothers. Sean is scribbling notes, but odds are good it's a recipe for grilled salmon, or maybe a dirty note to his fiancée.

Next to him is our brother Jonathan. It's the first time I've seen him since our dad's funeral, and it's freaking me out how much he looks like the late, great Cort Bracelyn. Same eyes, same hair, same jaw—hell, even the chin that looks like someone whacked him with a hatchet. Cleft, that's what it's called. Bree says he's good looking, and I can't argue with her.

But it's fucking eerie seeing the late Cort Bracelyn sitting across from me at the table. *Dad.*

My heart balls up in a painful knot, and it's not because I miss the old man. I mean it is, but that's not what's getting to me now as I think about dear ol' Dad.

It's the thought that maybe he wasn't. My dad, that is.

That's my big secret, okay?

Odds are good Cort Bracelyn wasn't really my father, even though he claimed me from day one. I've got a whole heap of reasons for thinking so, but I haven't said a goddamn word to anyone.

"Does that timeline work for you, Mark?"

I have no idea what James is asking, but I nod anyway. "Yeah. Sure."

"Great." The knowing look in his green eyes tells me he's not buying my act for one second, but he also knows I'm good at getting shit done. If he had doubts, he'd tell me.

"So, Bree, you can go ahead and let the media know about the senator's visit," James says as he flips to the next page. "Sean's already got a menu prepared, so from here we can move ahead with—"

Shit, what did I just agree to?

Ah, hell, it doesn't matter. I'd stay up for three weeks straight moving boulders with my bare hands if that's what my siblings said needed to happen. I'm committed to this resort thing, just like I'm committed to every person at this table, which is cheesy as hell. It's not like we grew up together. We're probably not even related.

I scan their faces, wondering how it's not obvious to everyone. How can anyone look around this conference room and believe the same guy sired all five of us? Yeah, we had different mothers, but everyone else shows signs of Cort Bracelyn's genes. Green eyes, where mine are brown. We're all hearty stock, but my brothers are more of that chiseled quarterback physique, where I'm more of a linebacker who swallowed a Mack truck. And that head tilt—they all do it when they talk, but I don't. Could be the boarding school thing, but I doubt it.

Who was the biological father?

Those are Chelsea's words, not mine, but they echo in my head now. We were talking last night about intrusive questions;

things customers ask as she fills their bakery boxes. I guess since she's dealing crack cocaine in the form of sugar-laced treats, people think they have the right to pry.

I bit my tongue instead of asking how she answers them, but damn, I wanted to know.

"That's lousy," I said instead. "Why the hell is it anyone else's business who supplied the batter if you're the one with the oven and the baking skills."

She laughed, quelling my fears that I'd just crossed some line. Polished, profanity-free communication has never been my thing, but I try not to be a dick.

"Oh, Mark," she said, voice shaking with laughter. "You're a funny guy. I wasn't expecting that."

Yeah, I'm a barrel of monkeys. Mister Personality.

Except with her, I almost feel like I could be. I've known the woman less than twenty-four hours, and I already feel like she gets me. Makes me a better guy. How the fuck did that happen?

"Are you on board with that, Mark?"

Jonathan's voice jars me back to the meeting, and I stare across the table into our father's face. His eyes are kind, and I'm sure he knows damn well I lost track of the conversation again.

"The plan to start phase three development early, if we hit our Q2 benchmarks next year," he prompts. "That good for you?"

Like I remember what the fuck phase three and Q2 are, but I nod and flip my packet until I'm on the page all the others are staring at. "Yeah," I say. "That sounds good."

"Why don't we take a break?" Sean suggests. "I can throw together grilled trout with roasted corn cream sauce, truffle au gratin potatoes, and some killer beet salad with arugula."

"Dear God." Bree pretends to swoon. "You're my favorite brother."

The rest of us ignore her, since she's bestowed that honor on each of us at one time or another.

Sean does a mock bow. "I can have it on the table in less than thirty minutes, and we can crack a bottle of Pinot."

That gets a frown from James. "We still have the financials to get through this afternoon. Everyone needs to be clearheaded."

"A *glass* of wine, James," Sean says dryly. "Not suggesting we bust out a case and start chugging straight from the bottle."

James sighs, but the rest of my sibs look damned relieved for the break. From across the table, Bree shoots me a smirk. "I have it on good authority that Mark's got a secret stash of cupcakes," she says. "Maybe if we're nice, he'll share."

Hell. That means she talked to Chelsea this morning, or maybe she just saw the bakery box yesterday. Anything's possible with my sister. She doesn't miss much, and she's always meddling in everyone's life. I'd be annoyed if I didn't secretly like it. Like that I'm part of something bigger, part of a family.

Don't fuck that up.

"Yeah," I say. "I'll grab the cupcakes."

I stand up and push away from the table. As I make my way to the door, I feel my siblings' eyes on me and wonder if they know I'm an imposter. That I'm not one of them.

That I'm scared shitless I don't belong.

* * *

THE MEETING finally wraps up about twelve-billion hours later, and my brothers and sister push back from the table like it's a prison break.

"Gotta run," Bree says. "It's girls' night."

Sean stops shuffling his papers into a pile and looks up. "That's right, my wife mentioned it."

He's not married yet, so I think he just likes saying the word "wife." Can't say I blame him. I've seen how he acts around Amber, and it's pretty damn sweet. Part of me envies the guy.

"You could have that, too, you know." Bree smirks at me, then

James, then Jonathan. In other words, the single brothers. "Just say the word, and I'll hook all three of you up with the town's most eligible women."

"No."

All of us respond in unison, but somehow my voice is loudest. Bree rolls her eyes, then pins me with *the look*.

"Just wait," she says. "One of these days you'll get bitten so hard by the love bug that you'll break out in hives."

James winces. "With an endorsement like that, I think I'll stock up on insect repellant."

"Ditto." Jonathan grabs his jacket off the back of a chair and looks at me with eyes so much like our dad's that the breath leaves my lungs. "You feel like grabbing a beer in town?"

I hesitate. It's rare to see Jonathan at all, since he spends most of the year running around the globe doing humanitarian work. Lately, he's used his yacht club background captaining a vessel in the Mediterranean, rescuing refugees fleeing horrific conditions in places like Libya and Tunisia. More than 23,000 people have drowned since 2000, but Jonathan's trying to change those odds.

He may be the spitting image of Cort Bracelyn, but in a lot of ways, he's Dad's polar opposite. Dad seized business deals by the balls and twisted, taking what he wanted out of life. The quintessential capitalist.

But Jonathan's using Dad's money for the greater good, putting himself out there to make the world a better place. I admire the hell out of him.

Plus, he's got the bloodline. He's not a fraud.

"How about Sunday night instead?" I suggest. "There's something wrong with the air duct for room one-seventeen. Gotta get it fixed before guests check in."

"Deal." Jonathan turns to James and Sean. "You guys in?"

"Sure." James shoves a stack of papers into a briefcase. "Can we make it later, though? I've got a conference call that evening with Senator Grassnab's team about the campaign launch."

"Need me to chime in?" Sean asks. "In case they have questions about the catering."

"Nah, we've got it covered."

"Excellent," Sean says. "I told Amber I'd bring Jonathan over for dinner that night. They haven't gotten to meet yet."

There's some muttering about bars and meetup times as my brothers amble away. Bree trails after them, both thumbs fluttering over her phone screen. When she reaches the door, she turns back to me. "Oh, hey, don't forget there's a light out in the Fireside Lounge."

Forget? I'm pretty sure she never mentioned it. "How many marketing VPs does it take to change a lightbulb?"

"Ha ha." She tosses her dark curls. "It's electrical, I think. Maybe you could take a look?"

"Yeah. Sure."

"Thanks." She smiles, and I know she's definitely up to something. "Sometime tonight would be awesome. There's a meeting in there first thing tomorrow morning."

"Sure," I mutter. "I'll do it after I tackle that air vent."

"You're the best."

She scurries off, still texting. Probably her fiancé, who was just promoted to police chief. Good guy, and I don't say that lightly. It takes a pretty kickass person for me to deem him worthy of my sister.

I wander back to my cabin and grab a sandwich, tempted to polish off the last of the cupcakes. But no, they'll be there later. Grabbing my toolbox, I head back to the lodge and take the stairs to the corner room with the air duct problem. The last guests complained it made a funny, wheezing noise when the heat kicked on, so I need to figure out what's up.

It doesn't take long.

"Son of a bitch," I mutter, snaking my arm into the vent to pull out a blueish-purple plush creature. A horse or a cow or something. I flip it over in my hands, remembering my own favorite stuffie as a kid. A dinosaur—brontosaurus, I think. My father bought it for me the summer I turned seven, and I came out to spend the whole month with him at the ranch.

"Got this for you since you're turning out to be such a big guy," he said, tapping the rim of my baseball cap. *"You're gonna be a tall one, aren't you?"*

I wonder if he knew then. If he suspected I wasn't really his kid.

Pushing aside the memory, I screw the cover back on the vent and pack up my tools. I shove the grungy stuffed animal under one arm, grab my toolbox, and trudge out of the room and back down to the first floor. Voices chatter from the direction of the Fireside Room, and I try to recall what Bree told me about the meeting tonight. I could have sworn she said tomorrow, but whatever. Might as well duck in and see if I can fix the damn light.

Halfway down the hall, I spot a crooked wall sconce. I can't just leave it, so I set down my toolbox and get to work tightening the screw. Once I finish, I notice the one across from it has the same problem, so I amble over with my screwdriver and get to work.

I'm almost finished when an eruption of female laughter stops me in my tracks. I glance toward the Fireside Room, where my sister's voice rings out plain as day.

"Girl, we need to get you laid."

Jesus.

I don't need to hear this. I edge back slowly, eager to reclaim my toolbox, as a female voice I don't recognize chimes in.

"Seriously, Chelsea—going too long without a big dose of vitamin D is bad for your health."

Chelsea? Wait—

I stop moving as another voice responds.

"Give her a break, Lily." That's Amber, I think. "Single moms have a little more on their plate than chasing dick."

Shit, that's what vitamin D means?

Which is hardly my biggest question here. Does Bree have more than one single mom friend named Chelsea?

I get my answer in the next breath.

"It's been a while, okay?" Her voice makes my whole body seize up. I stand frozen in the hallway, not sure whether to move backward or forward. It's *her*, and Christalmighty, I feel like someone's plunged my whole body into one of those warm chocolate fountains they have at weddings.

I hold my breath, waiting for her next words. I know that makes me a creeper, but I can't seem to make my legs move.

"Actually, you know what I miss?" Her voice is softly breathy, and I wonder if it's embarrassment or champagne.

"Orgasms induced by something that doesn't require batteries?" That's the other girl, Lily, I think. She sounds like a total firecracker, but it's Chelsea's voice I'm listening for.

"That, yes." Chelsea giggles, and it's the sweetest fucking sound I've ever heard. "Don't laugh, okay?"

"Oooh, this sounds good." My sister's voice is followed by the pop of a champagne cork. "No laughing, we promise."

"Okay, well." There's a splash of liquid in a glass, and someone —Chelsea?—takes a shuddery breath. "Not like I've hooked up with a lot of guys since I had Libby, or even before that—"

"Honey, we don't care if you've banged the whole town." Lily again, of course. "We're your posse. Your girls. Friends don't slut shame."

Okay, this Lily is growing on me. Not my type, but I love that she's got Chelsea's back.

"Right," Chelsea continues, voice still airy. "So, the couple times I've been with anyone lately, it's like they handle me with kid gloves. All gentle and romantic and afraid I'm going to break in half or something. Which is nice, don't get me wrong, but—"

"Sometimes you just want to be fucked hard."

Oh, Jesus. I did not need to hear my sister say those words.

I start backing up again, knowing I need to get the hell out of here. I've already eavesdropped too much and am in danger of being a serious stalker. I've almost reached my toolbox when Chelsea speaks again.

"Exactly! Like it's not going to offend me if we mix it up. Can you just do me doggie style or something?"

Holy crap on a cracker, I'm not hearing this. I mean I *am* hearing it, but I shouldn't be. I know that, but I can't seem to move away fast enough.

"I know a guy or two who'd be game for giving it to you a little rougher." Lily again, and I take back what I said about her growing on me. The thought of some other guy with Chelsea—

"Thanks, but flings aren't really my style," she says. "Anyway, I just met someone I think might have potential."

I stop again, boots glued to the slate floor. I should keep moving, but—

"Yes!" My sister claps her hands. "Please say it's my brother?"

My throat closes up, and I can't breathe. I grip the corner of the wall beside the stairwell, knowing I should make a run for it, but somehow my feet don't move.

"I plead the fifth." Chelsea's voice is coy and teasing and—getting closer?

Footsteps knock the slate floor, and I jump back into the alcove between the ladies' room and the stairwell.

But I'm not quick enough.

"Mark?" Chelsea stares at me. All the color drains from her face, and she brings both hands to her mouth as her eyes go wide as silver dollars. "Please tell me you didn't just hear that."

CHAPTER 5

CHELSEA

Please tell me you didn't just hear that.

My own stupid words echo back at me down the slate-tiled hallway, bouncing off the golden wood paneling and hitting me right in the face. Mark's expression is unreadable, but there's no way he didn't hear. I rewind the tapes in my brain, assessing the damage.

Can you just do me doggie style or something?

I close my eyes, willing this not to be real. What if he heard the rest—the part Bree said about her brother?

Dear Lord, this isn't happening.

I'm so focused on begging the floor to open up and swallow me that I'm startled when Mark clears his throat.

"I've been thinking about what you said." His voice is a low rumble, and I open my eyes to see him watching me. "About visiting the Humane Society to get a dog. Maybe this weekend."

Dog? Is this a doggie style joke?

But no, there's no hint of teasing in his eyes. Not even a smile. He's dead freakin' serious, and I can't tell if he really didn't hear what I said or if he's throwing me a rope.

I swallow hard, seizing the chance to pretend I said nothing filthy at all. Nope, just a casual chat with the girls about dogs and volunteer work and—

"What kind of dog are you wanting?" My voice comes out too loud, and I decide I shouldn't have had that second glass of champagne.

"Not sure."

I wait a few beats to see if he'll offer more, but I'm not disappointed he doesn't. If I learned anything about Mark in last night's marathon phone call, it's that he doesn't waste words. I never thought I'd admire that in a guy, but I do. Fewer words means less chance of bullshit, and I've had enough bullshit to last me a lifetime, thank you very much.

"Okay, let's see." I try to recall some of the questions they ask prospective pet adopters at the Humane Society. "Are you set on a big dog or a small one?"

"Size doesn't matter."

I will not look at his hands. I will not look at his hands.

Oh, Jesus, I looked at his hands. And yes, they're massive. Of course they are.

Color floods my face as I struggle to keep my eyes on his face and recall more dog-related questions. "What's your activity level?" I lean against the wood-paneled hall and wonder if he can tell I'm a bit unsteady on my feet. "Like are you looking for a dog you can hike with, or more of a lap dog?"

He considers that for a while, then nods. "Both, I think. I like being outside, but it's also nice to stay in."

How did I never notice how much these pet screening questions sound like the sort of things you'd ask on a first date? But hell, I may as well go with it.

"How patient are you when it comes to things like training and housebreaking and—"

—and women who are way out of practice at flirting?

"Patient." There's no hesitation in his response.

"You're sure? Some dogs require a lot of work."

He nods and rubs a hand over his beard. "First summer I visited my dad here, I fished the pond seven hours a day for a week before I caught anything."

"Okay, that's patient."

I file this information in the back of my brain, not sure what to do with it. I'm digging this opportunity to pepper him with personal questions, but I know I should stay focused on dog stuff.

"How about kids?" I ask. "Not that you have children now, but dogs are a long-term commitment. If you think you want kids in the next ten years or so, you don't want a biter or a dog that can't be around children."

That gets the tiniest smile out of him, and I'm sure he knows I'm fishing. God, could I be any more awkward?

"Even without kids, I'm not sure I want a biting dog," he says slowly.

"Good point. Okay, um—" I do a mental scan of the questionnaire, eager to keep putting conversational distance between Mark and what he may or may not have overheard at girls' night. "Are you looking for a puppy, or maybe a more mature dog that's had a home before?"

This question is key. Everyone loves a puppy, but it takes someone special to accept the baggage that can come with an older animal.

Or a single mom.

I urge my subconscious to shut up and wait for Mark's response.

"Used dog," he says.

"Used dog?" I catch myself smiling. "I've never heard that term, but I like it."

He shrugs and leans against the wall, bringing him infinitesimally closer to me. "Sorta like getting used jeans or books," he says. I'm struck by the rich brown of his eyes and the thought that a gazillionaire would buy any of those things used. "It's better when they're already broken in a little. When someone's flagged the good parts."

This is either the sweetest or most fucked up conversation I've ever had about late-in-life relationships. But we're not talking about relationships, we're talking about dogs. At least Mark is.

"That makes sense," I tell him. "Puppies are great, but they chew furniture and pee on the floor and have trouble sleeping through the night."

"How'd you sleep?"

"What?"

He smiles, and my insides turn to gooey caramel. "Last night. I kept you up late on the phone. Did you get to sleep okay?"

I nod like an idiot, charmed that he thinks he was the one who kept me up. Maybe I'm not the only one making more of this canine Q and A. "I slept great, thanks. You?"

"Like a baby."

"Or a used dog?"

The smile gets wider, his lips surprisingly full beneath that ruddy beard. "Exactly." He clears his throat. "Okay, what else?"

"Sorry?"

"What else should I think about when I pick a dog?"

I tuck some loose hair behind my ear, almost forgetting why I walked out here in the first place. I still have to pee, but I don't want to stop talking with Mark. I could stand here all night if my bladder let me.

"Breed," I say, remembering something else from the Humane Society forms. "Are you picky about getting a purebred or are you unconcerned with your dog's genes?"

Something flickers in his eyes. It's gone so fast I think I might have imagined it, and Mark takes his time answering.

"How much do you think genes matter?" he asks.

This feels like a test, but I have no idea what kind. My brain scrambles for an answer. Has he heard rumors about my daughter's father, or am I reading too much into this?

"It depends," I say carefully, not sure whether to answer from a canine standpoint or a human one. Maybe it's the same. "I guess sometimes there are medical reasons to care about genetics."

"Mpf," he says, and I have no idea if that's a good thing or a bad thing.

"But a purebred German Shepherd might have hip dysplasia bred into them," I continue. "And yeah, mutts can be unpredictable, but I saw this special once about how mixed breeds tend to have higher IQs."

"Yeah?"

"Yeah. Yes." I swallow hard, aware that the spinning in my head has nothing to do with champagne. His eyes are big, liquid pools of chocolate, and I feel myself leaning in. "So maybe the unknown is okay. Maybe that makes it better."

Mark stares at me for a long time. So long I wonder if he's going to say anything at all. I'm drowning in his eyes, in the fullness of his mouth, and I can't blame the champagne. I'm as clearheaded as I've ever been, and I want this man so much my chest aches.

"Damn." He breathes the word like a prayer, sending a shiver up my arms.

I lick my lips, not sure how to reply.

That's all it takes.

He reaches for me at the same time I step forward, and we crash together right there in the hall. I'm arching on tippy-toes, and he leans in to meet me, and our mouths find each other in a single breathless instant.

I don't understand it, but I don't need to. I don't care how a conversation about dogs can turn into this frenzy of heat and hunger. His mouth is achingly soft, surrounded by oceans of softness. I've never kissed a guy with a full beard, and all my senses flood with sensation. I'm spiraling into tickly softness, into a springy, silken cushion. I close my eyes, but open them again, needing to record this moment in my memory. What it feels like to lose myself in clouds of soft-spun energy.

He holds me against him, against a rock-solid wall of muscle that's such a contrast to the softness I gasp. He doesn't pull back, not like most guys who'd jerk away and inspect me for damage. It's obvious from the way I'm burrowing against him that I don't want him to stop. I'm practically climbing him like a tree, like a huge, burly, sexy tree.

His hand is rough in the curve of my waist, claiming me. There's a hunger in his kiss that stirs something deep inside me, something primal. He's not tentative, not timid, and I wonder again if he heard the conversation or that's just how Mark is.

That's just how Mark is I decide as he gives a low growl and deepens the kiss. I whimper and press into him, grinding hard against the front of his jeans. Some carnal creature has stirred awake inside me, standing up to stretch and growl and purr with pleasure. I drag my hands down his arms to claim those thick mounds of muscle. My fingers are greedy, devouring deltoids and triceps and a zillion muscles I never knew existed, much less in such grand scale. Good Lord, Mark Bracelyn is huge. And he kisses like a god. How have I lived this long without feeling such—

"Chelsea—oh, shit."

I jump back and whirl to face whoever's behind me.

Standing in the doorway of the Fireside Room is Bree, her expression a weird mix of fretful delight.

Mark curses behind me, but Bree moves forward.

"Whatever's going on here, I approve," she says. "And I hate to interrupt, but your phone's been ringing like crazy, and we were worried it might be your sitter."

Sitter. Libby.

I lick my lips and wonder if I'm the worst mother in the world.

"My purse—"

"Right here." Bree holds out my leather tote as my ringtone blares from inside. I fumble my phone from the inside pocket, hands shaking like I've just jumped on stage. Is that Mark's doing, or is it the sight of my babysitter's name on the screen?

I hit the button to answer the call. "Jody, hi, what's wrong?"

My heart thuds in my ears as I wait for her answer. Please, God, please let my baby be okay.

"Libby's fine," Jody says quickly. "We're both fine. But something's wrong with your car."

"My car?"

I glance toward the parking lot, which is silly. I took an Uber here tonight, wanting to be responsible. And Jody has her own car, so why is she—

"It's parked in the driveway where you left it," she continues. "But I heard this loud crash. Libby's fine, I checked," she says again, knowing I need reassurance. "But I looked outside and—"

Libby's fine. Libby's fine.

My brain is so busy chanting those words that I almost don't hear the next ones.

"—your car is kind of a mess."

I swallow hard, feeling Bree and Mark's eyes on me. I clutch the phone tighter, trying to understand what's happening. "Someone hit my car?"

"No, that's not it." Jody hesitates. "I don't think this was an accident."

"What do you mean?"

"Your window's smashed, and I think some of your tires are flat." She hesitates, like she doesn't want to say the words. "I think someone trashed your car on purpose."

"But—how—why—"

"I called you first," she says. "I wasn't sure if I should call the cops or—"

"Call the police," I tell her. "I'll be right there. Thank you for calling, Jody."

If I thought my hands were shaking before, they're doing double-time now. It takes me three tries to get the phone back into my purse, at which point I yank it right back out again because now I need an Uber.

"What's wrong?" Bree asks. "Did something happen to Libby?"

Mark steps around me, forehead etched with concern. "How can I help?"

My heart is pounding in my head, but it does a little surge at Mark's words. There's nothing like male protector instinct, and it means more coming from this giant of a man. This giant of a man who kisses like a dream and whose hands were just—

"I need an Uber," I tell them as I toggle to the app. "Someone vandalized my car, but Jody and Libby are fine. I just need to get home right away before—"

"I'll drive." Mark grabs the phone from my hand, and I'm too stunned to resist.

"But—"

"You're not going home alone." He slips the phone back into my purse with hands way steadier than mine.

"I won't be alone, I'll have an Uber driver," I protest feebly. Truth is, I'll feel a whole lot better if Mark's with me. "And Jody's there with—"

"No." Mark shakes his head, and there's so much steel in his eyes that I clamp my mouth shut. "First someone fucks with the door at your shop, then someone rings your doorbell late at night. Now this?"

I clamp my mouth shut. Dear Lord, is he right? Could those things possibly be connected?

Bree's staring at me with concern. "Is that true, Chelss? Is someone messing with you?"

"I can't imagine those things would be linked." My words sound weak, like I don't believe them myself.

I look up at Mark, strong and capable and so damn sexy I lose my breath.

"Okay," I tell him. "Thank you. Take me home, please."

He nods and pulls a set of keys out of his pocket. "Let's go."

CHAPTER 6

MARK

It's past nine when I pull into Chelsea's neighborhood, and my heart is just now slowing down. I tell myself it's the scare of knowing someone fucked with her car, but I know damn well that's not it.

Jesus, Christ, that kiss.

"Can you think of anyone who'd want to mess with you?" I force myself to stick with the subject at hand.

"No." Her voice is soft, and I glance over to see she's biting her lip. There's fear in her eyes, but I don't know whether to blame the dickhead who trashed her car or something else. What isn't she telling me?

"Right here," she says, and I ease up to the curb in front of a small brown house with gray trim. Two massive pots of yellow flowers flank a brick-red door with a glass panel running alongside. It's probably pretty, but right now, it looks more like a safety hazard. *Hell.*

I scan the whole front yard, noticing thick, flowery bushes that anyone could hide behind, and a driveway that's only dimly lit by one small bulb. Bad guys could be lurking anywhere.

She reaches for the door handle, but I catch her hand in mine.

"Wait." I glance down at my phone. "Austin will be here in two minutes."

"Austin? You called the police chief?"

"Bree called her fiancé." Who happens to be the police chief, so yeah. "Humor me," I tell her. "I'll feel better knowing someone I trust has checked it out."

Before she can argue, a police SUV pulls up behind us. There are lights mounted on top, but Austin's smart enough not to turn them on. The last thing Chelsea wants is a scene. A police cruiser car pulls up right behind that, and the cops get out and confer with each other.

Chelsea has the door open on my truck before I'm totally unbuckled, and she's already talking to Austin by the time I reach her side. "I'm sorry to bother you; I'm sure everything's fine."

"Not a bother at all. It's good to see you, Chelss." He nods to me. "Mark. Everyone, this is Officer Studebaker."

There's some grunting and nodding and other pleasantries as we shake hands and meet the young-looking cop beside Austin. The whole thing feels weird since we're all standing in the driveway in the dark.

Chelsea wrings her hands in front of her. "Thank you all for coming," she says. "I'm sure this is all just—*oh my God.*"

All of us gasp as Austin trains the beam of his flashlight over her car. *Holy shit.*

The cops take a few steps forward to survey the damage. Glass litters the driveway, sparkling like water as they flick their lights across an ocean of it. All four tires are slashed to ribbons, and there's something scrawled across the front windshield. I glance at Austin and see his jaw is rigid.

When he meets my eyes, I know damn well what he's telling me.

Get her inside.

Chelsea shivers, giving me a good excuse. "Come on." I slide an arm around her shoulders, surprised at how chilled she is. "Let's get you warm and let Austin do his job."

"But—"

"I'll join you in a minute," Austin says, grabbing a radio off his belt. "I've got some questions for you."

I'm guessing he means Chelsea and not me, but I can't read much more in his expression. Chelsea looks like she wants to resist, then deflates. She lets me lead her to the front door, hands shaking as she unlocks it.

"Chelsea, thank God." A young woman with purple streaks in her hair greets us at the door, then steps aside so we can enter a well-lit living room. I'm guessing this is the babysitter. "I didn't know what to do."

"You did the right thing," Chelsea assures her. "Thank you for calling me."

"No problem." The girl waves as a pair of headlights swing into the driveway behind us. "There's my mom. She insisted on coming. Um, do the cops need me?"

"I'm not sure." Chelsea glances back to where both of them are peering at the windshield. At the *words* on the windshield. What do they say?

"Could you check with them before you leave?" Chelsea asks. "Oh, I almost forgot—"

Chelsea fishes into her purse and pulls out three twenties. Damn, is that how much babysitters cost? The single mom thing is no joke.

"Thank you for being here, Jody," she says. "Sorry for the scare."

"No worries. Call if you need anything."

The girl hustles out the door toward her mother, who's already deep in conversation with the cops. Chelsea waves to both of them, then stands there helplessly for a second. A chilly breeze whips up, rustling the leaves on the willow in her front yard, and making Chelsea's coppery hair flutter around her face.

"Come on," I tell her. "Let's get inside where it's warm."

"Okay." She doesn't move.

Shit. What would my sister do? Or my mom. "Maybe we should have mint tea or something."

"Mint tea?" She blinks at me like I've suggested knocking back shots of molasses. "Oh. Yes, good idea." She puts a hand in front of her mouth and huffs a breath. "I probably still smell like champagne?"

Shit. That's why she thinks I want mint?

"No." I'm damn familiar with the taste of her mouth, the sweetness of her breath. It's not champagne at all, and I'm hungry to taste her again. "Mint tea's good with honey."

"Mint tea and honey." She gives me a weak smile as I pull the door closed behind us. "That would be a good cupcake flavor."

"My mom made it for me," I say. "When I'd have a bad dream."

"Your mom sounds sweet."

"She is."

Chelsea glances down a long hallway. "I'd better check on Libby. You want to wait in there?"

She gestures toward an oversized purple couch before scurrying off down the hall. I think about offering to make the tea, but the last thing she needs right now is some oversized dumbass banging around in her kitchen. I turn toward the living room and survey the cluster of ferns by the window, the fuzzy blanket the color of warm oatmeal, the framed photo of a pig-tailed little girl. The place is cozy, like my mom's living room.

It was a room a lot like this one where my parents sat and had the conversation. The one they didn't know I could hear, hunkered where I was behind my mom's big fern in the corner. I'd gone there to grab my stuffed dinosaur, but I stuck around when they started speaking in hushed tones.

"If you won't marry me, then at least take this." My dad's voice was a weird mix of gruff and kind.

My mom gave a soft gasp, and I peered over the edge of the

pot to see her handing him something. "No one needs that kind of money for child support," she whispered. "We're not some charity case you can buy off, Cort."

My father mumbled something low under his breath, and I caught a few words I wasn't allowed to say. Dirty words, my favorite kind. When my dad spoke again, his voice was low. "He's my kid. I take care of my kids."

"Cort." My mother folded her arms over her chest and frowned. "We don't even know for sure he's yours."

"He's mine."

"But—"

"He's *mine*, goddammit."

My mother's face was tight, and she didn't answer right away. "Fine. Have it your way. But if he ever asks—"

"He's my kid."

She sighed. "If he asks, I'll be honest."

I never asked. Not once, not even the summer after I turned fifteen when an envelope showed up at my dad's ranch. I handed it to him with the rest of the day's mail, pretending I didn't see the return address marked "DNA Labs Incorporated."

It could have been anything. God knows my father was generous about spreading his DNA around.

"What's that?" I asked casually, hoping he couldn't hear the interest in my voice. Hoping he didn't know how much I'd wondered.

"That," he said, picking up the envelope and scowling at it. He ripped it in half, then ripped it again and again until all that remained was a pile of confetti. He grinned and met my eyes again. "That, my son, is bullshit."

I never asked about it again. Yeah, maybe I went back and dug the paper shreds from the trash, rummaging through his desk for the tape. I thought about doing it. Piecing those words back together and getting answers once and for all.

But in the end, I chickened out. I lit a fire out back and tossed the confetti in one great big handful.

Even then, I was a great big coward. Cort Bracelyn might have been a philandering asshole who couldn't keep his pants zipped, and he wasn't even that great a father. But he was *my* father, and I loved the son of a bitch.

If I'm not Cort Bracelyn's son, then who the fuck am I?

Clearing my throat to shake myself back to the present, I aim myself at Chelsea's overstuffed purple couch. I settle on one end of it, careful not to knock off any of the fuzzy throw pillows or disturb the pile of stuffed animals arranged in a semi-circle. The tiny plastic dishes on the coffee table suggests Chelsea's kid had a tea party of her own.

"Here you go." Chelsea moves into the room with a tray holding a yellow teapot and four small mugs. Extras for the cops, though they're still outside waving flashlights around. A third cop has joined their party, and I suspect they may be a while.

"Thank you." I take one of the cups from Chelsea, conscious of how small and breakable it is. I look up to see her studying my hands, and she takes a few breaths before meeting my eyes again.

"Honey?" she says.

My breath stalls in my chest. "What?"

A nervous laugh bubbles out of her. "For your tea." Her cheeks flush as she scoops up the plastic honey bear and hands it to me.

Shit.

I take the bear and try to pretend I knew that all along. That there wasn't a fleeting moment where I thought we'd gone from kissing in a hallway to calling each other pet names.

"Thanks." I squeeze about eight tons of honey into my mug, then set it back on the tray.

"You've really got a sweet tooth, huh?"

"Yeah."

Scintillating conversation, dumbshit.

I rifle through the trash heap in my brain for something to say. "You've got great cupcakes."

Chelsea grins, and it dawns on me that sounded like some pervy comment about her tits. Or a request for cupcakes. Either way, it sounded rude.

"Which one tasted best?"

I'm still hung up on the boob thing, so I take a few beats to answer. "The pineapple," I tell her. "And the coconut and caramel one. Hell, they're all amazing."

Her smile gets bigger. "I'm glad you liked them."

I take a sip of the tea. It's like syrup with a little mint flavoring, which is just how I like it. I drain half of it in one gulp and wonder who the hell invented these itty-bitty cups.

Chelsea gives me a shy smile. "Is that the way your mom makes it?"

I nod. "Yeah. It's good."

"I had peppermint and spearmint, and I wasn't sure which you liked." She shrugs, fidgeting like she's nervous. "It probably doesn't matter with all that honey in it, huh?"

"Probably." God, she's sweet. And I'm an idiot who can't carry on a conversation. I swipe a hand over my beard. "My mom's the opposite. Can't stand sweet tea."

"How about your dad?" she asks. "Did you get your sweet tooth from him?"

I swallow hard, tasting honey on the back of my tongue. "No."

She's still looking at me, and I know I owe her something more. A thank you for the tea at least. "My mom had a lot of boyfriends."

Now where the hell did that come from?

Chelsea doesn't bat an eyelash, though. "Was that hard on you?"

I set my tea on the tray, sloshing a little over the edge. I have no idea why I brought that up, and no idea how to get out of talking about it now.

See? This is why I don't share shit.

But I opened this can of worms, so I might as well throw a few of them at her.

"Sometimes," I say. "I mean, single moms deserve a life, too, right?"

"Of course." She sips her own tea. "Not at the expense of their kids' happiness, though."

"It wasn't like that." Not exactly. I wonder if Chelsea noticed my single mom comment. "My parents never got married."

"No?" She looks surprised. "I'm sure she had her reasons."

Now that's interesting. Most people who hear that figure it was my dad's call. Philandering billionaire knocks up a school teacher and pays her off so he doesn't have to marry her.

But it wasn't like that at all. Not even close.

"She never wanted to get married," I say. "Called marriage a trap."

"Harsh." She cocks her head to the side. "Have you been married?"

"No." Big shocker.

I want to ask her about herself. I want to know everything about her, down to where she buys powdered sugar and what sounds she makes when she comes.

But I remember what she said about people at the bakery asking nosy questions, so instead, I refill my tea and keep my dumb trap shut.

"I haven't been married, either," she says. Her gaze flicks to the front window as blue and red lights flash outside. So much for the cops playing it cool.

When Chelsea looks back at me, her eyes are troubled. "Sorry I tried to argue about you bringing me home," she murmurs. "I didn't think it would be that bad. I didn't think—I guess I've never had anyone destroy something of mine like that."

There's a part of me that's aching to pull her into my arms and kiss her again so she stops looking like I ran over her puppy. But that's the last thing she needs from me right now.

"Any idea who'd do this?"

She looks down into her lap. "No. Not really."

"Not really." That's not the same thing as *absolutely not.*

I wait for her to say more, but she's as tight-lipped as I am. Fair enough.

Her hands are folded on her knees, fingers interlaced like she's holding herself together. I hesitate, then reach over and cover both her hands with one of mine.

She looks up again, and I hold her gaze. "I know there's stuff you keep to yourself," I say slowly. "I've got things like that, too."

She looks at me for a long moment. "Okay."

"Do me a favor when Austin comes in here," I tell her. "Be straight with him. I'll leave the room if you want, but he needs to know if there's something that'll help him catch who did this."

She nods again, then bites her lip. "I dated him."

"Who?"

"Austin." She glances toward the door. "That's not a big secret or anything. Bree knows about it, and it isn't like we were serious or anything. I just—I wanted you to hear it from me. In light of—um—"

The fact that we were all over each other less than thirty minutes ago?

She's got nothing to worry about if she's thinking I'll be jealous. Not my style.

"Austin's a good guy," I tell her. "You have good taste."

She smiles, and I wonder if she took that as some kind of ego stroke. She kissed me, after all, so does that mean I'm a good guy?

"I don't, actually," she says, and it takes me a second to find my place in the conversation. "Have good taste in men? I—um—the thing is, I haven't always made great choices."

I keep my eyes locked on hers, waiting for her to continue. It's okay if she doesn't want to. She owes me nothing, but I find myself wanting to hear more. To understand what makes Chelsea...well, *Chelsea*.

"I'm sorry," I tell her. "Do I need to beat anyone up for you?"

She laughs, but there's something stiff in her laughter. A hint that I may have struck a nerve. "See, that's the thing. This guy I dated before Austin—Charlie? He, um. Well, he turned out to be —that is, he—uh—he hit."

"Son of a bitch." Rage flares under my breastbone, hot and dangerous.

"It only happened once," she says quickly. "And I left right away after—"

"Where is he?" My hands ball into fists on my lap. "I'll kill the bastard if you say the word."

She looks at my hands, then shakes her head. "It won't be necessary. He's in jail. Not for the abuse, though it did turn out he had a record for it."

"I hope he rots there."

That gets a stiff smile out of her. "Thank you." She presses her lips together. "Anyway, he wasn't the only one. I mean, he was the only one who hit me—it was just the one time. But there were other men, guys who weren't all that nice." She takes a shuddery breath and gives me another forced smile. "I wanted you to know that. My judgement, it hasn't always been so great. It's kind of a flaw."

"Sounds like you're not the one who's flawed."

Her blue eyes flash. "I am, though. I pick the worst guys and think I can fix them. That they'll become better, that they're really good people deep down."

"You have a kind heart," I tell her. "That's not a flaw."

"Thank you." Her smile seems steadier this time. "For what it's worth, my taste seems to be improving."

I'd like to think she means me, but I'm probably kidding myself.

"We both have histories," I tell her. "Unless yours includes serial murder or rooting for the Yankees, it doesn't change how I think about you."

The edges of her mouth tug up, the first full smile I've seen since we got here. "You think about me?"

Busted.

"Yeah," I admit. "I do. But before we go too far, I should tell you that I—"

Ding-dong.

God dammit.

Chelsea flies off the couch and runs for the door. She throws it open to reveal Austin there arguing with the younger cop.

"—you don't ring the doorbell when there's a kid sleeping," he snaps.

"It's okay, come in," Chelsea says, ushering them inside. "I need to check on Libby, though. Make yourselves comfortable."

She's gone before I can say anything, so I stand there staring at the cops. I jerk a thumb at the sofas, figuring that's what she means by comfortable. "Have a seat."

"Thanks." Austin folds himself into an armchair upholstered in cream and purple stripes, while the younger cop—Studebaker?—takes a seat on a loveseat that matches the sofa. I hesitate a second, not sure whether to sit or stay standing.

But cops aren't fans of big shaggy-looking guys towering over them, so after a few beats, I settle back on the couch. I put my hands on my knees where they can see them, aware of the murmured voices down the hall. Chelsea's kid must've woken up.

"Mark is Bree's brother," Austin says by way of introduction. "Studebaker's new to the force."

No shit.

I nod in acknowledgment and glance at the door. "You've still got someone out there?"

"Dusting for prints." Austin clears his throat. "You were with Chelsea when her sitter called?"

I wonder what the hell Bree told him. *"Mark had his tongue down Chelsea's throat"* sounds about right.

"I was at the lodge," I say. "So was Chelsea."

Austin nods and leans back against the armchair. Anyone who didn't know him might assume he's just phoning it in, that he's not taking this seriously. But I know Austin, and I know this posture is the one Bree calls Casual Cop Mode. The guy knows what he's doing. "Bree mentioned there'd been other incidents."

I glance toward the hallway and wonder how much to say. It's not my place to tell Chelsea's story.

But it is my place to say what I've witnessed, so I do. I tell them about the fucked-up door, and about the ding-dong-ditch thing last night. Somewhere in the middle of that, younger cop takes out a notepad and starts jotting. Austin keeps his eyes on me, his expression steady and unflinching.

I'm wrapping up my account when Chelsea walks back in with a fresh honey bear. Shit, I emptied the other one.

"Sorry to keep you waiting," she says as she pours tea for the cops and hands them each a cup. "Sounds like Mark filled you in on everything?"

"Yes, but we'd like to hear from you." Austin glances at me, and that's my cue to stand up again.

"I can wait in my truck," I say. "Or in another room."

"No, stay." Chelsea puts a hand on my arm, and I glance down to see her eyes are wide and fretful. Under the happy hostess front, she's scared as hell.

I drop my ass back down on the sofa and settle in next to her. She leans close, and I feel how cold she is. I pull the oatmeal colored blanket off the back of the sofa and arrange it around her shoulders.

"Thanks," she murmurs, then looks at the cops. "Let's see. The door at the shop was messed up when I came in the other morning. Monday, I think?"

"Has this happened before?" Austin asks.

"No." Chelsea bites her lip and glances at me. "The ding-dong-ditch thing has, though. Three or four times, maybe?"

That's more than she told me about, but I don't react.

Neither does Austin, not visibly anyway. "It's always at night? The doorbell ringing, that is?"

"Yes." Chelsea looks down at her hands. "I thought someone was trying to scare me. Kids or something."

"Do you keep cash at the shop?" Austin's voice is velvety smooth and unthreatening. I'm grateful he knows what he's doing.

Chelsea shakes her head. "No. Not here, either. I didn't—" she glances at me. "I didn't think the stuff at the shop could be connected to the doorbell stuff here. Not until tonight."

Austin nods and splays his hands over the arms of the chair. "Is there anything else you can tell us? Ideas about why someone would want to scare you?"

Chelsea looks up, trying to meet Austin's eyes. She holds for only a few breaths before her gaze skitters away. "No." She shakes her head. "Not that I can think of."

Austin looks at me. I'm positive he didn't miss that, Chelsea's lack of eye contact. Something's up, but I don't think any of us are going to find out about it right now. Not tonight anyway.

Austin probes again, gently. "Any names you can give me, anyone who'd have a beef with you?"

I think about what she told me, about her history of dating lousy guys. Is that what Austin's fishing for?

Chelsea shakes her head. "No one comes to mind."

There it is again. That slight skittering of eye contact.

Austin doesn't comment, but I'm sure he noticed. He stands up, so we do the same. "For now, I'd suggest installing some motion-sensor lights out there. Maybe security cameras."

Chelsea frowns. "That sounds expensive."

I shove my hands in my pockets. "I'll do it."

She gives me a sharp look. "I can't ask you to do that."

"You didn't," I point out. "I volunteered."

She bites her lip. "My car," she says softly. "I have to be at the Humane Society at eight in the morning. Libby and me, it's our volunteer shift. We can't miss it."

Austin rubs his chin. "The guys at McCormick's Auto Shop are fast, but maybe not that fast," he says. "I can put in a call, but—"

"I'll take you." I don't give her a chance to argue. "I'm going anyway, to get a dog."

Chelsea's eyes widen, but Austin just nods. "Good idea. In fact, it might be smart for you to stay here." He glances at Chelsea. "If it's okay with you, of course. You've got a guest room?"

Chelsea frowns. "Yes, but—" she glances down again. When she looks up, her eyes are troubled. "You think there's a risk he'd come back?"

He.

Was that a slip, or just a logical guess that anyone who'd do something this lousy must have a penis? I don't ask, but I can see Austin filing the observation in the back of his brain.

"We don't know what we're dealing with yet," he says slowly. "But we do have one more question for you."

"What's that?" Chelsea's hands are clenched in her lap, and I wish I could reach over and unspool the tight knot of her fingers.

Austin glances at Officer Studebaker, who starts to speak in a nervous burst.

"The words written on your windshield," Studebaker says. "Shoe polish or motor oil or chocolate or something. McCormick's should be able to get it off, don't worry."

"It's the words themselves," Austin says, his jaw tight. "That's more our concern."

Beside me, Chelsea stiffens. "What do they say?"

Austin stares at her, no expression on his face. "Keep your mouth shut." He clears his throat. "So, let me ask one more time—any idea who might have done this?"

CHAPTER 7

CHELSEA

"Sorry it's so small." I look up at Mark, not sure how his massive frame is going to fit on this tiny double bed in my guest room. "It really wouldn't take me more than five minutes to change the sheets on my bed, and then you could have a king-sized—"

"No." He folds his arms over his chest. Huge arms, tree-trunk arms, arms capable of protecting me if it comes to that.

Jesus Christ, how has it come to that?

Keep your mouth shut.

I swallow hard, wondering if I should have done exactly that with the police. I didn't tell them anything useful. Not really. Just a hunch, but maybe that's enough.

"That was brave," Mark says softly, and I wonder if he read my mind. "What you told the cops back there."

I look down at the comforter, smoothing the duvet so I don't have to meet Mark's eyes. "I don't know it was him. I haven't heard from Charlie Crawford for years."

Admitting out loud that I dated a guy who hit me—once, that was all it took before I got out—was awkward enough. Admitting it in front of a guy who looks capable of dismembering him for it was another matter.

"I was stupid," I murmur now. "I was only twenty, and I thought if I just left, that would be enough. I didn't think to report it, and that was wrong. I know that now."

God, I feel dumb. Dumb for falling in love with a guy like that. Dumb for not filing a report. Dumb for thinking if I just moved away, he'd vanish from my life for good. He did, or at least I thought so. Now I'm not sure.

"Hey." Mark's voice is low and soft, and his eyes match that softness when I meet them. "None of this is your fault, okay?"

I nod, even though I don't believe him. "Okay."

"Hey," he says again, stepping closer. I feel the heat of his body, the solidness of his presence, and I can't help meeting his eyes. When I do, my core turns to warm honey. "I mean it, Chelsea. You're not to blame for someone else being an asshole."

This isn't the first time someone's said that to me. Having a strong pack of girlfriends and a history of choosing lousy men made sure of that.

But something in Mark's voice, in his eyes, makes me almost believe it. I nod because I can't find any words, but maybe I don't need them. My memory flickers with the feel of that beard rasping soft and gentle against my face.

I want that again. I want *him*.

I swear he reads my mind again. His arms slide around me, pulling me in for a hug. A comforting squeeze, I'm sure that's all he means to give me. But I tilt my face up at the last second, and our mouths pull together like magnets.

"Chelsea." He says my name on a growl the instant before his lips meet mine.

Then we're kissing, kissing fierce and frantic like two starving people. I claw at his shirt, craving his heat, his strength, his whole damn body. The plaid flannel is warm, and so is the cotton undershirt beneath it, but the heat in his clothing is nothing compared to what I find when my fingers tunnel under it. Flesh, hot and solid and taut with muscle. This massive wall of a man is like a playground for my hands, and I clutch greedily at his bare back.

He groans as I stroke my palms up his spine, memorizing the feel of his shoulder blades under the heels of my hands. My God, there's so much muscle. So much coiled energy hiding just under the surface.

Mark makes a low rumble in his throat and clutches me tighter. His tongue strokes mine, a kiss that's rough and possessive and exactly what I need right now. Both hands cup my face, but he lets one drop to my waist. I urge him on, grinding against the hardness behind his fly to tell him I want more.

His palm starts moving, slow and steady, up my ribcage. I know where he's headed, but still gasp out loud when his palm cups my breast. I practically melt when his thumb strokes my nipple through the thin cotton of my shirt.

I've never wanted anyone this much in my life. It's not even a want, it's a need. If I don't feel this man inside me in the next five minutes, I'm going to lose my mind.

"Mark." His name comes out in a gasp against his mouth as my nails dig into his bare back. My whole breast fits in his hand, and I'm aching for him to rip my bra off with his bare hands. With his teeth if necessary, I just need more. The huge pad of his thumb circles my nipple, and my knees start to buckle.

I take a step back, pulling him with me toward the bed.

But it's like pulling the leash of a dog who doesn't want to walk. He stiffens and breaks the kiss. When he draws back, his eyes are full of fire.

"I can't."

What?

I glance at the front of his jeans. I can't help it; I know damn well he *can.*

"That's not what I meant," he says, shifting a little so the bulge is less apparent. "I mean we shouldn't," he clarifies. "You've had a rough night. And I don't want to take advantage."

"You're not taking advantage." The words come out hoarse and desperate. "I'm a big girl, Mark. I know what I want."

He closes his eyes, looking pained. "I can't."

I open my mouth to beg. I'm not proud, I want this guy so badly my whole body aches. It's more than just a physical urge, though that's powerful enough to knock my knees out from under me. I need his sweetness to erase the bitter fear inside me. I crave his bigness to make me feel less small and afraid.

And yeah, I want him. *Badly.*

But what kind of jerk would I be to plead with a guy who's clearly telling me no? If the tables were turned, if I were the one resisting, he'd be an asshole for trying to change my mind.

My brain understands this, but the greedy clench between my thighs tells me the rest of my body isn't getting the message.

He opens his eyes and takes another step back. His movements are shaky and forced, and I can tell it's taking as much strength for him to back away as it's taking me not to reach for him.

"You don't know how much I fucking want to," he says, scrubbing a hand over his beard. "But this isn't—I can't—I won't—"

"I get it." I don't, totally, but watching him fumble like this is painful. And staying here in this room just ups the odds that one of us will snap.

I edge sideways, doing my part to put distance from us. To keep myself from reaching for him. The bed is right there, but so is the door.

I choose the door.

"Good night, Mark."

With that, I turn and run.

* * *

I'M up early the next morning.

It's partly to make sure I've got time to explain to Libby about our houseguest, and partly because I hardly slept a wink. I was too keyed up, too aware of the sexy, virile, hot-as-sin man sleeping just down the hall.

How would he have responded if I'd gone to him in the night? If I'd slipped naked into bed with him, pressing my body against the hard, hot length of his.

Don't be an idiot.

That's what I told myself last night, and again this morning as I tiptoe past the guest room. The door is open, and I can't resist peeking inside.

But instead of a glimpse of Mark, I see the bed made up neatly, throw pillows arranged exactly how I had them before. The smell of coffee pulls me toward the kitchen, where I find a freshly-brewed pot and a note scrawled on a sticky note in a thick, blocky hand.

CHELSEA,

Figured it's best if I'm not here when Libby wakes up. Will be back with breakfast by 7:30.

M

I RUN my fingertips down the paper, oddly touched that he called Libby by name. Not *your daughter* or *the kid*, but *Libby*. Her own person, not an extension of me.

Most guys don't do that. Not that I've dated tons of them in the six—almost seven—years since Libby was born. But the few who've made it past a first date have been cautious and itchy, referring to my child in abstract terms instead of as a real person.

And the guys I dated before that—well, let's just say I've picked some real winners. Charlie Crawford, the guy who forgot to mention he'd gone to jail once on an abuse charge. My college boyfriend Antonio, who neglected to tell me he had a fiancée back in Brazil. Matt Carmichael, who spent six months claiming to be a lawyer from Portland, when he actually ran an illegal cockfighting ring in Scio.

And then there was Libby's father…

I glance back at Mark's note and feel my balled-up heart unclench.

"Mommy?"

I look up as Libby pads into the kitchen all sleepy-eyed and rumpled. She's changed out of pajamas and into a pink and yellow tutu over blue jeans with a red and gray plaid work shirt I bought for her when we started our volunteer shifts at the Humane Society.

"We're going to help the puppies and kitties today," I remind her as she fluffs the tutu. "Is that what you're wearing?"

She frowns, then scurries back toward her room. "I forgot my tiara," she yells from down the hall.

All right, then.

I pour myself a cup of coffee and wonder what Mark meant by breakfast. Should I cut up fruit or maybe fry bacon?

I hear the rumble of his truck's engine before I see it, and my heart speeds up in an embarrassingly Pavlovian response. The battered blue and white truck wheels into my driveway, which is when I realize my car is gone.

What the hell?

I scramble to the front door and yank it open, stepping onto the porch as Mark's getting out of the truck. "Did they take my car for evidence or something?"

He shifts a big pink bakery box to his other arm and slams the truck door. "Nope." He ambles up the walkway, not even pretending he doesn't notice I'm braless under the thin cotton tank I'm wearing. *Good.*

"Then where—"

"Figured it might upset Libby to see your car all bashed up," he says. "I had McCormick's come out with a tow truck early this morning. And then I got donuts."

Holy cow, he's been busy. And hungry, judging from the size of that donut box.

"Thank you for thinking of that," I say. "All of it. The towing, the donuts—everything. I'll pay you back, of course."

Mark frowns. He's standing less than a foot from me now, and I watch the lines deepen on his forehead. "Let's get something straight." His voice is rough, but not unkind. "When my dad died, he left behind a fuck-ton of money. More money than any five humans could possibly spend in a lifetime."

I lick my lips, aware that he's sharing way more personal info than he owes me. "You don't have to—"

"Since I'm one of those five humans, and we're equal heirs, I've got a ridiculous shit-wad of money that I don't particularly need," he continues like I haven't spoken. "If I sometimes want to share with friends and family and people I care about, I'll damn well do it."

I hold his gaze with mine, looking deep into those dark brown eyes. "Which am I?"

His brows furrow. "What?"

"A friend or someone you care about."

His eyes stay locked with mine, not blinking at all. "You have to ask?"

"I—"

His arm ropes around my waist before I say more. He closes the space between us with a soft growl and claims my mouth. The kiss is possessive and hungry and leaves zero doubt this is way more than friendship.

I grip the back of his neck and thank the Lord I had the foresight to brush my teeth already. I kiss him back hard, pressing my body against his to let him know I'm ready to pick things up where we left off last night. My body hasn't stopped buzzing since then, and I'm so mind-whacked I'd cheerfully let him bend me over the porch rail right now. That's how badly I want him.

"Are you mommy's boyfriend?"

I jump back, totally busted, and try to look like mom instead of some hussy making out on her front porch at daybreak. I turn to face my daughter, tugging down my tank top before crossing my arms over my chest.

Libby peers up at me with innocent eyes, her tiara askew on her head. She's still wearing the tutu, and has added a pair of glittery high-top sneakers to her ensemble.

"Hi, baby." I clear my throat. "This is Mark, and he brought us breakfast."

Mark steps forward, presenting the pink box with humble reverence. "Donuts." Spoken like a man who fully grasps the distraction power of sugar. "Two dozen. I wasn't sure what everyone likes."

"Donuts!" Libby claps her hands together and does a happy little twirl in the doorway. "Come on, we've got milk."

She scurries into the house, leaving the door open behind her. Mark and I look at each other.

"Thank you." I don't know if I'm thanking him for the kiss or for the donut distraction, but either way he nods.

I follow my daughter into the kitchen with Mark keeping a safe distance behind me. With any luck, Libby's forgotten her boyfriend question.

No dice.

"Mommy doesn't have boyfriends," she chatters happily as she pours milk into three mismatched mugs, sloshing some on the counter. "I can't have a boyfriend until I'm thirty."

Mark looks at me and nods. "Sounds about right."

"But I can get my ears pierced when I'm ten," she continues as she puts the carton back in the fridge with the cap still sitting on the counter in a puddle of milk. "And when I'm eighteen I go to college. Oh! And when I'm thirteen I can watch Farrah Spewler."

"Farrah Spewler?" Mark looks mystified.

"Ferris Bueller's Day Off," I say. "Some older kids at school told her about it. It's PG-13."

He sets the donut box on the table and scrubs a hand over his beard as Libby sets a mug of milk in front of him. "That's a lot of rules," he says. "Your mom's really smart for knowing them all. And you're smart for remembering them."

"Yeah." Libby's eyes widen as Mark opens the donut box to reveal a huge assortment. "You got the good ones."

"Boston cream?" Mark accepts the plate I hand him, but keeps his eyes on my kid. Like this is his favorite conversation all week. "Or are you a maple bar kinda girl?"

"No, jelly." Libby jabs a chubby finger at a berry-filled confection in the corner, smudging powdered sugar all over her hand.

"Libby," I warn. "What did we talk about last week? About touching food that doesn't belong to us?"

Mark stays silent, and I can see him doing his best to keep his face fixed in a serious expression.

Libby's doing the same. "You touch it, you eat it," she recites, grinning at me. "And if I lick it, it's mine."

The corners of Mark's mouth twitch, and I can tell he's avoiding my eyes. "Sounds about right."

We each choose a donut—jelly-filled for Libby, a maple bar for me, Boston cream for Mark. He polishes his off in two bites and reaches for another, cinnamon sugar this time. That's gone in less than thirty seconds, leaving him studying the box like a cigar aficionado admiring a display of fine Cubans.

Libby looks up in awe. "You can eat a lot of donuts."

"My mom says I have a stomach like a cow," he says. "Multi-chambered. Even if the dinner chamber gets full, there's always room in the sweets chamber."

My daughter's eyes go wide. "I think I have that, too," she says. "A cow stomach."

I point to her milk. "Work on that. Then we'll talk."

She gulps it down, eyes fixed on Mark like he's the most fascinating creature she's ever seen.

As I pick at my donut, I acknowledge she has a point.

CHAPTER 8

MARK

"Mark Bracelyn! Oh, my goodness, it's you."

The greeting when I walk into the Humane Society is so effusive that I look behind me to see if there's some other Mark Bracelyn. Maybe a sports hero or a rock star.

But no, the woman's looking right at me with her salt-and-pepper perm gleaming under the animal shelter's florescent lights. She launches herself like a bespectacled missile, throwing her arms around my middle in a grandmotherly hug.

Who the hell is this woman?

"Mrs. Percy," Chelsea supplies helpfully. "It's good to see you. How did your event go for the Children's Welfare Society?"

Ah, got it. She's one of the charity ladies Bree's always helping with big donations and free event space. That explains the warm welcome.

"I'm here for a dog," I say as Mrs. Percy loosens her grip on my midsection and gets to work hugging Libby and Chelsea.

"How wonderful," she chirps. "Are you thinking big dog, little dog? How about activity level or age?"

I glance at Chelsea, amazed to realize it was only last night we had this conversation. I never did ask her about that doggie style comment I overheard.

The pink flush in her cheeks tells me I'm not the only one thinking about that. I tear my eyes off her face and will myself to stop thinking about it.

"Uh, no preference," I say. "Just a dog."

"We're surprisingly short on dogs right now," Mrs. Percy says, consulting a clipboard on the counter. "We've got four of them out at PetSmart right now for an adoption event, and two are out on walks with volunteers. But if you head through that door right over there—"

"Mom. *Mom*!"

Both Chelsea and Mrs. Percy turn around, though it's obvious who Libby's talking to. She's kneeling on the floor in front of a cage too small to contain any dog I've ever seen.

"Look." Libby points into the cage. "They've got a rabbit."

"Don't put your fingers in the cage, honey." Chelsea moves toward her, and I'm struck once again by how good she is at this mom thing. How she knows stuff like ears get pierced at ten and don't stick your hands in rabbit cages.

I follow her to the corner, curious about the rabbit thing.

"He came in about a week ago," Mrs. Percy says. "The usual story, I'm afraid. People who buy bunnies for their kids' Easter baskets don't think about the challenges of having a pet rabbit. So many of them end up here when it turns out they're more work than a stuffed animal."

I drop to my knees beside Libby and peer through the bars. Inside the cage is a creature five times the size of the little field rabbits we have out at the ranch. He's white with splotches that looks like someone spattered him with black paint and a little cotton-puff tail with a brown tip. His ears are floppy like he can't be bothered to hold them upright, and he lies sprawled with his hind legs flat behind him and his arms outstretched. Put a cape on him, and he'd look like a superhero bunny in flight.

Libby's downright delighted. "Mommy, can I pet him?"

Chelsea bites her lip, and I wonder how Lib decides when Chelsea is "Mom" and when she's "Mommy." I make a note to pay attention, and also to go visit my own mother soon. It's been almost a month, and we haven't talked yet this week.

"He's friendly," Mrs. Percy says behind us. "Neutered and litter box trained."

"Litter box trained?" I peer at the rabbit. I didn't know that was a thing.

"Neutered?" Libby scrunches up her nose and studies the other end of the rabbit.

"That's where they cut off his boy parts to make him behave better," Mrs. Percy offers helpfully. "To make him a nice boy."

Chelsea tries unsuccessfully to stifle a laugh while Libby turns her attention to me. "Did it hurt?"

"Did what hurt?"

"You brought us donuts, so you're nice," she says. "Did it hurt when they cut off your boy parts?"

Oh, Jesus—

Chelsea's flat out laughing now, not even trying to hide it. I do my best to wrangle the conversation back to safer territory. "When they neuter dogs or cats or rabbits, they uh, make them fall asleep first so it doesn't hurt," I offer. "They do it so they can't make more dogs or cats or rabbits that don't have homes."

There. That was good, right? A safe explanation with no curse words or graphic details. Hopefully age-appropriate, though Chelsea's laughing too hard to weigh in.

Libby cocks her head at me. "How are babies made?"

Uh-oh.

"Um—"

"Libby." Chelsea pulls it together and musters up a stern tone. "You know the answer to this. We have that book, *How Babies Are Made*."

"Well yeah, but I wanted to see if *he* knows."

Libby studies me like a schoolteacher issuing a quiz. I have no idea how to respond, but I know I can't look at Chelsea.

"Yeah," I manage. "I—um. I think I've got a handle on it."

"Are you *sure*?"

"Pretty sure."

"Because if you want I could let you read the book."

"Thanks?" I look at Chelsea, not sure how to change the subject.

She wipes the laughter tears from her face and puts two fingers through the bars of the rabbit cage. "Let's pet him."

Good distraction. Libby obliges, wriggling most of her fingers through the bars to stroke a spot near the rabbit's hind legs. "Ooooh," she breathes. "He's so soft."

"He is, isn't he?" Chelsea smiles. "Even softer than kittens and puppies."

Damn.

The sweetness on her face makes my chest ball up tight. What is it about this woman that turns my insides to goo?

I can't get more than a finger through the bars, but it's enough. Enough to stroke a spot behind the rabbit's ear, and holy shit, they're right. This bunny has the silkiest fur I've ever felt. I've never touched anything this soft, and I've touched plenty of soft things.

Chelsea.

I command myself not to think of her, not to remember the way her breast curved into my palm last night. God, she felt amazing.

I shake my head, trying to clear the X-rated image from my brain. For fuck's sake, I'm in an animal shelter with a mother and her child. What kind of perv has dirty thoughts in a place like this?

"You should get him." Libby's small face is scrunched with seriousness. "He might be better than a dog."

I hold Libby's gaze, wondering where she got her eye color.

Hers are more hazel to Chelsea's blue, but they have the same upturned nose and soft sprinkling of freckles. The kid is so achingly sweet that it hurts my teeth to look at her.

Never in my life have I thought of myself as a future dad. Blame it on the whole notion of "dad" getting mixed up in my brain, but I never imagined myself as one.

But sitting here now, bonding with this little person over bunnies and donuts and the fact that we both really dig her mother, there's a tiny voice in the back of my head.

What if?

"I know!" Libby claps her hands together, breaking the spell.

"You know what?" Chelsea asks.

"I know what we name him."

"The rabbit?" Chelsea looks at me. "No one's said they're getting the rabbit. Mark hasn't even seen any dogs yet."

But I know I'm getting this rabbit. I don't need to see any dogs.

"His name," Libby continues like her mom hasn't spoken, "is Long Long Peter."

We stare at her. Even Mrs. Percy—who's been silent for the last few minutes—is staring in dumbfounded amusement. "I beg your pardon?" she asks.

"Long Long Peter," Libby repeats with obvious impatience. "Peter, like Peter Rabbit."

"Oooh-kay." Chelsea's not looking at me, and I'm guessing she's on the brink of another laughter explosion. "But Long Long Peter?"

"Because he's stretched out long," Libby says, gesturing to the bunny like we might have missed it. "Long Long Peter."

"Can't argue with that." I turn and look at Mrs. Percy. "I'll take the rabbit, please."

* * *

"You got a freaking rabbit?" My sister looks at me like I've just told her I got a tattoo of Mickey Mouse on my ass. "I thought you wanted a dog."

"I changed my mind."

She shakes her head and watches Long Long Peter hop through my living room, pausing to inspect my sofa for edibility. "He's cute," Bree says. "I thought it was some kind of weird euphemism when you called me to bunny sit."

James gives her a pained look from his spot against the wall in my entryway. "And you agreed without knowing what the euphemism meant?"

Bree shrugs and takes a slug from the grape soda she confiscated from my fridge. She makes a face but doesn't put down the can. "So, I'm just supposed to make sure he doesn't chew cords or poop anywhere, right?"

"Yep."

Long Long Peter hops over to James and sniffs his shoe. My brother stiffens but doesn't draw back his shiny-looking loafer. "You're sure it doesn't have rabies?"

Bree rolls her eyes. "We're not sure *you* don't have rabies, but we keep you around."

I glance at my watch and wonder if Jonathan and Sean are already at the bar. We agreed to go separately to guys' night, since those two were having dinner at the reindeer ranch with Sean's fiancée, Amber, and her sister, Jade. Jade's engaged to our cousin, Brandon, so he's there, too, and might even join us for guy's night.

Bree's got an odd little scheming look on her face, and I wonder if she's plotting to fix Jonathan up with one of her friends. Or James. She already worked her magic on me, even though I'm fighting it. Even though a relationship is so not what I need right now.

"We should go," I tell James.

"Agreed." He tosses his car keys from one hand to the other. "Not that I'm not riveted by your pet bunny."

His tone is cool and aloof, but I heard him baby-talking the bunny when I was in the kitchen putting rabbit pellets in a bowl. James might look like Mister GQ, but deep down, he's an endearing dork.

I turn back to Bree, who's stooped down petting the rabbit. "Thanks for watching Peter."

Bree quirks an eyebrow. "You mean Long Long Peter?"

I have yet to use his full name, which means Bree's been talking to Chelsea. I wonder what else Chelsea mentioned. The kiss? Er, kisses, plural? Or the fact that I copped a feel when—

"Relax, big guy." Bree straightens up and elbows me in the ribs. "I'm not asking her about your sex life. My job was to get you together. What you do from here on out is your business."

"I thought your job was to annoy the crap out of us," James says dryly.

"That, too." She grins and sips her soda. "You really should get some pop that's not pure sugar."

"Why?" I honestly can't fathom that.

"Come on." James starts to turn, but Bree grabs his tie and yanks him back.

A tie. Seriously. To a fucking guys' night.

"Call if you need a ride," she says. "Seriously. If anyone has more than one beer—"

"Relax, Bree." James extracts his tie from her claws and smooths it out. "I'm the designated driver. We're fine. Have a good night."

He turns and strides out the door, making a beeline for his black BMW. I hesitate in the doorway and turn back to Bree. "Is it just me, or does that guy need to get laid?"

She laughs and bends down to scoop up Long Long Peter before he can scuttle out the door. "Look who's talking." She plants a kiss on my rabbit's forehead and steps back into the entryway. "Come on, bunny nephew. Let's watch some *Animal Planet*."

I pull the door closed behind me and follow James out to the car. I sling myself into the passenger seat, touched to discover he jacked it back to make room for my legs.

"Thanks for driving."

"No problem." He shoots me a wry look as he eases out of the parking spot. "In case you hadn't noticed, I like being in control."

I study my brother, a little surprised by the sharing. We're not super close, James and me. Hell, I'm not sure he's close with any of us. He's the oldest Bracelyn spawn, raised by his mother somewhere in New York. That and his former life as a high-powered attorney makes us as different as two brothers can be.

Maybe not even brothers...

James clears his throat and steers us onto the highway. "So, Mark." He clears his throat again. "Are you happy being part of the management team?"

I stare at him, baffled by the question. His eyes stay fixed on the road, and his posture is ramrod straight. What the hell?

"What the fuck are you talking about?"

He doesn't flinch the way I expect him to, the way some people might. I guess he's gotten used to me in the two years we've spent getting the resort up and running.

"I mean, are you comfortable in a management role?" James says. "Do you like what you're doing for Ponderosa Resort?"

I stare at my brother, suspicion creeping into my chest. "Is this your way of kicking my ass to the curb?"

"What?" He jerks so hard the car swerves. I fight the urge to reach for the wheel, remembering what he said about control. "Are you crazy?" He tears his eyes off the road and gives me a hard look. "Even if I could fire you—which of course I can't, you're one of us—why on earth would I do that?"

You're one of us.

The words echo in the darkness of the luxury car, and I

wonder if he hears them, too. If he recognizes the uncertainty of them.

"Sounded to me like you're driving at something," I say. "Like maybe you think I don't belong."

I wait for him to say it. To acknowledge what we both suspect. He must know something, right?

"Jesus, Mark." He shakes his head and hangs a sharp left on the road leading into town. "All I'm asking is if you like the administrative stuff. The meetings and numbers and business plans."

"You're asking if I like meetings?"

"I know you hate meetings." He gives a dry laugh. "I know you'd rather shove bamboo under your fingernails and soak your hands in grapefruit juice than attend another strategy session. That's why I'm asking. If you'd rather avoid that part altogether."

What's he saying? Is he looking for a tactful way to cut me loose, or is he genuinely gauging whether I'd prefer a different role with the company?

I stare at the side of his face, wondering if I'd be able to read him better if we'd grown up together. If we'd met each other more than a handful of times when our visits with Dad overlapped.

"I like being part of things," I say carefully. "The business. The family."

James takes his eyes off the road again and looks at me like he's discovered a grizzly bear riding in the passenger seat of his car. "Of course," he says. "You'll always be those things."

Will I?

I don't ask the question out loud, but I'm sure he sees it in my eyes. Maybe now's my chance. Maybe I should call out the elephant in the room. Maybe we'd all be better off if we stopped pretending.

"James." Fuck, I'm not sure how to say this. "Have you ever thought maybe I'm not—"

Bzzzzz!

God dammit.

I jerk my phone out of my pocket, ready to shut it off or maybe throw it out the damn window. The flicker of Chelsea's name on the screen stops me in my tracks. She knows I'm with my brothers. Unless it's an emergency, she'd never call.

"Hello?" My heart is hammering in my ears.

"Mark?" Her voice is small and shaky, and I grip the phone tighter. Something's wrong.

"What is it? Are you okay?"

There's a sharp intake of breath—a sob or a sigh?

"I'm okay," she says. "But someone broke into my house."

CHAPTER 9

CHELSEA

I'm in the living room talking with Austin when Mark shows up at my house. He knocks twice, then bursts through the door with fire in his eyes.

"Are you okay? Where is he? Where's Libby? Are you hurt or—"

"I'm fine." I'm still shaking, but I'm okay. More than okay, now that Mark's here. My chest floods with warmth at the sight of this giant of a man looking so shaken over—me?

It's clear he's not buying it that I'm fine. He scrapes a hand over his beard and turns to Austin. "Is she really all right? Did he hurt her or—"

"No." Austin shakes his head. "Not physically. She's had quite a scare. I'll let her tell you about it."

I already gave him the broad strokes on the phone. How I got home from dropping Libby at a sleepover and walked into the guest room to find a man rifling through my file cabinet.

I left out the part about going in there in the first place so I could sniff the pillowcase Mark slept on. He doesn't need to know I'm a creepy loser who's hooked on the scent of his soap.

I also left out the details of how terrified I was when the

intruder turned to face me. Blue eyes. That's what I remember. He wore a ski mask that hid the rest of his features, but not the shock in those icy blue eyes. He wasn't expecting me home so soon, and certainly didn't expect to be caught with his hand in my file cabinet.

"What are you doing?" That's all I got out before he pushed past me and ran for the door, flinging it open like the house was wired to explode. He left it gaping open in the wind, tires screeching in his wake.

Thank God Libby wasn't here.

And thank God Mark is here. I've never been so grateful to see anyone in my life.

"You're not staying alone tonight." He looks at Austin. "Back me up on this."

Austin looks at me, hesitating. "I agree it's not a good idea for you to stay here alone, but we could—"

"I'm staying." Mark folds his arms over his chest. "Or we're going to my place. Take your pick."

I should be annoyed by the whole commanding, alpha-male thing he's doing, but mostly I'm relieved. "I could drive to Prineville and stay with my mom," I point out before remembering that won't work. "Except Libby's getting dropped off here early in the morning, and anyway, I don't want the house unattended if that guy comes back."

Not that I have much to steal, but still. My skin crawls at the thought of a stranger prowling my home, touching my things, while I'm off sleeping in a lumpy twin bed at my mother's house.

"Guest room's still free?" Mark asks.

"Yes."

"Good." He nods at Austin. "I'll stay. I won't let her out of my sight."

I don't ask how he plans to do that if he's sleeping in the guest room, but I'm too rattled to ask questions. I want to hurl myself against Mark's chest like a big, fat baby and let him wrap those tree trunk arms around me 'til I stop shaking.

"But you have your guys' night with your brothers," I protest. "I don't want to interrupt that."

"They insisted," he says. "A woman in distress trumps bro time. It's in the rule book."

"How did you even get here?"

"James dropped me off," he says. "And Bree's rabbit sitting."

And Mark made sure I got my car back this afternoon, so he really has thought of everything. I bite my lip and look at Austin. "Is it okay if I check the file cabinet to see if anything's missing?"

He nods. "We already checked for prints. Got a couple latents we'll run through the system. You're pretty sure he had gloves?"

"One glove," I remember as a flash of memory shakes loose in my brain. "He must have taken the other off to flip through papers in my files."

Austin nods and makes a note on a little pad in his hand. "We'll see what turns up when we run the prints. Go ahead and check to see if anything's out of place."

I nod and turn away to shuffle slowly down the hall. My legs are shakier than I thought, and I stop halfway to grip the closet doorframe and keep my bearings.

I'm standing there just out of sight when Mark's voice rumbles low in the living room. "You checked on this Charlie guy who hit her?" he asks. "The one who's in jail?"

There's a long pause before Austin responds. He's a by-the-rules kind of cop, and I'm sure there are privacy regulations about this.

"I was sitting right next to her when she told you about it," Mark reminds him. "The last time you were here."

Austin clears his throat. "I told her this right before you got here," Austin says slowly. "He's out."

"What?"

"Out of prison," he says. "It was almost a year ago. He was

doing time in Idaho for fraud, so it never even came up on our radar."

Mark curses low under his breath. "So, he's out there just roaming around?"

"It would appear so." Austin's voice is low, and I wonder if he knows I'm lingering here in the hallway listening. He doesn't miss much. "What's she told you about him?" he asks.

"Enough to know he's a fucking asshole." The words are a deadly-sounding growl. "And not the only asshole she dated." He pauses. "Not you."

Austin laughs out loud, which covers the sound of my own soft snicker. "Thanks," he says. "And that answers that question."

"You mean whether I knew you two dated?"

"Yeah." Another long pause, and I wonder if I should stop eavesdropping. This is a man to man kinda thing, not my business. But it *is* about me, and besides, I'm pretty sure Mark eavesdropped on girls' night Friday, so this makes us even.

I press my hand against the wall and strain to hear their lowered voices.

"We weren't serious," Austin says quietly. "I'm sure she told you that, but I wanted you to know—brother to brother—things aren't going to be weird if you're dating."

"Dating." Mark repeats the word like it's a foreign language. "Shit. That's not—I'm not—we aren't—"

Austin's laugh is louder this time. "Don't bother," he says. "You know I'm trained to spot when people are telling the truth and when they're full of shit. It's written all over your face that you're nuts about her."

Is it? I can't see Mark's face, but his voice sounds softer than normal. Uncertain, which is something I've never heard from him. "It's complicated," he says. "My mom, she was a single mom, too. It's confusing as hell for a kid to have new 'uncles' jumping in and out of their lives, you know?"

"Chelsea's not like that," Austin says. "Not even close."

"I know," he says. "I mean, I could have guessed. All the more reason not to fuck that up for her, right?"

Austin doesn't answer right away. When he does, he's so quiet I can barely hear him. "Maybe you should let her be the judge of that."

"Maybe." Mark sounds utterly unconvinced, and I don't blame him. Why on earth would he trust my judgement when I've made it clear I don't trust it myself? I flat-out told him I've got a track record of making bad choices with men. Hardly an enticement for him to be next in line.

There's some more murmuring, but I can't make out the words. I've already been gone too long, so I duck into the guest room and make a beeline for the file cabinet. Yanking open the top drawer, I survey the contents.

Credit card statements. Health insurance info. Records from the small business loan that helped get Dew Drop Cupcakes off the ground. Nothing seems to be missing, though it's possible the guy snapped photos of things. Is that all he was after?

No, wait—

I pull out the folder, an unobtrusive one marked "Libby keepsakes." Wasn't this in the bottom drawer before?

I can't be sure, but I clutch the file to my chest and make my way back down the hall. Mark and Austin are still talking, and they both look up when I enter.

"What did you find?" Austin asks.

"I'm not sure." I lay the file folder on the coffee table and flip it open. "I can't be positive, but I'm almost sure this was put back in the wrong drawer."

Austin frowns and looks down at the image on top of the file. It's Libby's baby picture, a photo of her curled against my chest in the hospital with her tiny pink fingers clutching a fistful of my hair. Beneath that, the edge of her birth certificate peeks out, one edge crinkled.

He looks back at me. "May I take a look?"

"Of course."

I sit down on the sofa and watch him shuffle through the contents. Mark hovers protectively beside me, frowning down at the folder. "You thinking identity theft?" he asks as Austin pauses on the birth certificate. "Someone looking for social security numbers or something?"

"Not sure." Austin keeps flipping, past the little card onto which I've taped a curl of hair from Libby's first haircut.

The sight of it makes my heart clench. "I always meant to make a baby book for her," I say softly. "That's what most of this is for."

A wave of guilt washes through me, and I wonder if I made a mistake keeping Libby to myself. Thinking I could do it alone as a single mother. Maybe—

"Can you tell if anything's missing?" Austin looks up at me.

I shake my head. "I don't think so, but I can't be sure." A forced-sounding laugh moves through my chest. "I'm not even positive I didn't move the folder myself. Maybe when I was reorganizing last month. It's not like I look through it all that much."

Even as I say it, I know it's not true. I'm almost a hundred percent certain I never moved that folder. Why would I?

The quizzical look I get from Mark is a good indication he's thinking the same thing. He doesn't say anything, though. Neither does Austin.

When Austin finally stops shuffling through the folder, he looks up at me. "You're sure you didn't recognize the guy?" he asks. "His build, his eyes, maybe his clothing?"

"Positive." That much is true.

Austin closes the folder. "I'll ask you this again in case something's jogged your memory," he says slowly. "Can you think of any reason someone would mess with you or Libby?"

This is my chance. My opportunity to say something. To give words to the tiny sliver of doubt wedged in the back of my brain.

Instead, I shake my head. "I don't think so." I hesitate. "You said you haven't been able to track down Charlie? Charles Crawford, I mean."

Austin looks at me moment. "Correct. His last known address is in Idaho."

Mark scowls and lowers himself to the seat next to me on the couch. His massive thigh bumps against mine, and I lean into it, needing his solid heat.

"Has he tried to contact you?" Mark asks.

"No." I shake my head again. "Not for years." I bite my lip. "He did send me a letter, though."

"When?" Austin asks.

"Two years ago?" I shake my head. "He was still in prison. Maybe three years."

"What did it say?"

"That he missed me." I shiver at the memory, hugging my arms around myself. "How did he put it? That he was 'sorry things didn't work out.'"

"Instead of 'sorry I fucking hit you?'" Mark's voice is a snarl again.

"Right." I glance at Austin, but he's got his impassive cop face on. "Anyway, there was some stuff about wanting to get back together. I didn't think much of that at the time. But he suggested this date idea, this plan to take Libby and me to the High Desert Museum."

Austin studies me. He's a good cop, so it doesn't take him long to put the pieces together. "He went to prison four years ago," he says. "Libby's almost seven."

"Exactly," I say. "So how did he know about her?"

Austin stands up and flips the folder closed. "Do you mind if I take this with me?"

"Be my guest," I tell him. "I'll get it back, right?"

"Right." He moves toward the door, and I stand up to accompany him, but my legs don't want to work. I stand there like an idiot with my knees quivering and my hands still shaking. Have they ever stopped?

Behind me, Mark shifts so his leg braces mine. I wonder if he knows he's lending me his strength.

At the door, Austin turns back to us. "Keep everything locked," he says. "If you decide to stay here tonight, I'll have a patrol car swing by a few times."

"Thank you." I shove my hands in my back pockets, feeling silly and scared. "Tell Bree I said hi."

"Will do."

As soon as he's gone, I feel myself wilt a little, but I fight to keep my spine stiff. "You don't have to babysit me," I tell Mark. "I can go to my mom's place, seriously."

"Do you want to go to your mom's place?"

I bite my lip. I have to be honest. "Not really. I'll just have to listen to her lecture me about living alone, about getting pregnant in the first place."

God, I sound pathetic. I clamp my mouth shut to stop the flow of words, but Mark doesn't look like he's judging.

"And you'd rather be here than at my place?"

I hesitate, then nod. "If Libby got scared or sick and needed to come home early, I'd want to be here. And if the guy really was planning to come back, he'd think twice if he saw my car in the driveway."

And the six-five mountain man in my guest room.

I don't say that part out loud, but maybe Mark knows it.

"Then we'll stay here," he says. "I'll stay here. With you."

This is where I'm supposed to argue, right? I should stamp my foot and cross my arms and insist I'm a strong, independent woman who doesn't need a man to protect her.

I wonder if Mark sees this monologue scrolling on the teleprompter in my brain, because he reaches down and takes my hand. "Hey." His voice is a low murmur as he laces his fingers through mine. "It's okay to let someone else watch your back. You do everything else yourself. Let me help, Chelss."

That undoes me. The softness of his voice, the strength in his fingers, the truth in his words. Even the way he says my name—all of it dissolves something in the center of my chest.

I don't realize the tears are coming until I feel one slip down my cheek. My whole body starts to shake, and I wonder if it's the shock wearing off.

Mark looks rattled for a second, and I wonder if he's one of those guys who can't handle a woman crying. But then he pulls me into his arms and somehow guides me to the couch. He settles down next to me so I'm practically on his lap, and the solid, flannel-covered heat soothes me almost instantly.

He doesn't say anything, that's the crazy thing. Just strokes one big hand down my hair over and over, holding me tight against his chest until the shaking stops. He must feel it the same instant I do, because he loosens his hold on me. I look up into those warm brown eyes and take a deep breath.

"Thank you."

He nods but keeps his arm around me. "You want tea or Kleenex or something?"

I shake my head. "Just this. You holding me a little while longer if that's okay?"

"Of course."

I take a shaky breath and look down at a frayed spot on the knee of my jeans. "I just keep thinking 'what if Libby had been here?' And what kind of mother am I if maybe I did something that brought this into her life?"

Mark jerks back like I've stuck my finger up his nose. "Are you fucking nuts?"

Well that's one way to comfort a woman.

"No, I just—"

"Chelsea, listen." He shakes his head with such incredulousness that I almost feel bad for questioning my own mom instinct.

"You're a fucking amazing mom, and I say that as a guy raised by one of the greats."

"Oh." Okay, that *is* actually comforting.

He's quiet a while, but I sense he's not ending the conversation. That he's thinking about how to say something. "You know what's great about you?"

I have no idea. "Um—"

"The way you just *know* what's the right age for Libby to date or get her ears pierced or watch certain movies."

I laugh, taken aback that he's chosen to focus on that of all things. "I might be kidding a little with some of it. She'll probably have her first kiss before thirty."

"But that's what I mean—your instincts, they're superhuman."

I stare at him, not sure what to make of this compliment. It might be the sweetest thing anyone's ever said to me, and he doesn't even know the truth. That I spend half my time as a mom doubting myself, wondering if I'm doing it right. I struggle to find my voice. "I don't know about that."

"What's the right age for a kid to make her own bed?"

I blink. "Four. Depends on the kid, but for one like Libby, four or five."

"How about pouring milk instead of having a grownup do it?"

"Somewhere between five and six." He noticed that? That I let Libby do it herself, even though she didn't get it perfect, because it matters to her that I trust her with grownup tasks.

"How about Santa?"

I look up. "You mean learning he's not real?"

"Santa's not real?" His voice is so deadpan that I'm startled for a second. The flicker in his eyes gives him away.

"Of course, Santa's real," I tell him. "The tooth fairy, too. But around age ten or eleven, it's time to have a talk about how grownups have played that role for generations, and now that she's becoming a grownup, she's let in on the secret and can help perpetuate the magic."

Mark smiles, and I feel like a kid who's gotten a test answer right. I'm honestly just winging it with some of this, but knowing I have the answers—even imperfect ones—is making me less shaky.

And turned on.

I'll be honest, the way Mark's holding me right now is making me feel less like a mom and more like a flesh and blood woman. A flesh and blood woman pressed up against a rock-hard, solid, sexy as hell man.

"Right age to learn about the birds and the bees?"

I jump at his voice and answer without thinking. "Young," I say. "Four or five for the broad strokes of how babies are made, but it's an evolving conversation. Especially when they're teenagers or young adults."

"Right," he says. "I guess 'penis' and 'vagina' mean something different when there's a chance you'll see real ones instead of cartoon pictures in a book."

Holy shit.

Okay, I have this theory.

Men who get weird about using real, anatomical names for body parts stand a good chance of being closed-off and prudish in bed. Same goes for shock-value words like "cock" and "pussy" and "fuck." If saying it out loud makes a guy squirmy, he'll probably be squeamish about *doing* it.

But a guy who rattles off words for body parts without flinching? That's a man who knows how to use those parts.

Not that I've lab-tested this with thousands of subjects, but I've experimented. Let's just say my theory is batting a thousand.

"You okay?" Mark asks.

"Yeah, why?"

"You stopped breathing for a second."

"Oh."

I glance down and see my hand has somehow found its way to his thigh. I decide to leave it there and lift my eyes to his again.

"I—um—was thinking," I tell him. "Curious how old you were the first time you—"

I trail off there. It's not that I'm hung up on words like "sex" and "virginity." It's just that we're inching into uncharted territory. Are we friends who've kissed a couple times, or something more intimate? Have we earned the right to ask prying questions, or is that crossing a line?

Mark shifts on the sofa, and my hand slips a few more inches up his thigh. I stare at it, aware that my fingers are lying there scant inches from the fly of his jeans.

I clear my throat and try my question again. "How old were you when you, um—"

"Found out about Santa Claus?"

His tone is deadpan, but when I look up, he's smiling. With his arm around my shoulders, he leans down and brushes the gentlest kiss on my forehead. "Seventeen," he says.

"Oh."

"Assuming Santa is a code word for having sex?"

"Um—"

"Because seventeen's a fucked-up age to still believe in a bearded fat man forcing his ass down the chimney to bring presents."

"Right." I giggle unexpectedly. "I was eighteen."

"Yeah?"

"Yeah. It was—good, actually."

I hold my breath again, waiting. Is that a threat to his masculinity? Am I supposed to pretend I've had only lousy sex because I'm waiting for someone like Mark Bracelyn to sweep me off my feet and show me the key to multiple orgasms?

"I'm glad." Mark brushes his lips across my forehead again, and I swear I could have one of those orgasms right now. "I like knowing you've had good stuff mixed in there with the not-good stuff."

My heart.

God, it feels like it's going to bust right through my rib cage.

That's not the only body part throbbing at the moment, but I order myself to hold it together. To keep this conversation going.

"Dating," he says softly.

"What?" I look up at him again, and there's definite heat in his eyes.

I can't help it. I slip my hand up his thigh just a fraction of an inch. Not enough that I'm grazing his fly, but enough to watch his eyes flash.

"What's the right age for dating?" he asks.

"Sixteen." I'm just throwing that out there, positive we're no longer talking about my daughter. "That's alone in a car with a boy, but group dates are okay a few years before that."

"How about things that happen on dates?" His voice is huskier than it was a few minutes ago, and I shift my hand another fraction of an inch.

"Such as?" My voice sounds funny, too, breathy and a little flirty.

"Hand holding."

"Hand holding is nice."

"Hmm." He reaches for my hand, the one that's not grazing his junk. Lifting it to his mouth, he plants a soft kiss across my knuckles. He releases it and lets his palm come to rest on my shoulder. "How about touching?"

I lick my lips and remind myself to keep breathing. "Touching where?"

I shift my hand another half-inch and watch his eyes flash.

"Breasts." His hand glides to mine and I gasp. His fingers curl possessively around it, thumb skimming my nipple. The moan slips out as I press myself into his palm.

"Yes, please." I move my hand a good three inches this time, no longer pretending I'm not going for his button fly.

Mark curses under his breath as my knuckles graze the hard length of him. Good Lord, he could pound nails with this thing.

"Chelsea." He says my name on a strangled groan, and I look up to see his eyes are troubled.

"Yeah?"

"I'm not having sex with you."

"Wh—why not?" I try my best to keep the disappointment from my voice, but I fail miserably.

"Because you've had one helluva scare tonight," he says. "And I don't want you to regret anything."

"I swear I won't."

He smiles and shifts his hand to my other breast. The squeeze is rougher this time, and I know we're not stopping. That's not what he's telling me.

"There will come a time when I slide hard and deep inside you," he murmurs. "Any way you want it. You said something about liking it from behind?"

Jesus Christ, I'm drowning. Drowning in my own desire. I can't see straight. Can't hear over the buzzing of lust in my brain. I can't speak. All I can do is nod.

"But not tonight," he says.

I want to throw myself on the floor and scream like a toddler. I'm so keyed up that I swear I could come by crossing my legs. But that's not what I want. I want Mark. I need his touch, so desperately I can't sit still.

Maybe he sees it in my eyes. Or maybe he's as worked up as I am. Looking into his eyes, I'm startled by the wildness there. He's as hungry as I am, and he's not hiding it.

"I need to taste you," he says. "Please, Chelsea."

I'm pretty sure he's not talking about cupcake samples.

I can't breathe. Is he seriously begging to go down on me? I'm nodding before my brain processes the words, and that's all it takes. Mark scoops me into his arms and picks me off the couch. His legs don't even wobble, and I feel like I'm made of air as he carries me toward the front door.

"Where are we going?" I breathe.

"Deadbolt." He takes one hand off my ass and flips the lock, keeping me cradled in his arms the whole time. Then he moves across the living room and down the hall.

"Which room?"

"Left," I pant. "End of the hall."

My bedroom door is half open, and he kicks it wide with his boot. Then he's tossing me back on the bed, his mouth claiming mine with a hunger that leaves me clawing at his back. His beard is soft and rough at the same time, as he kisses his way down my throat, across my collar bones.

Somehow, I get my hands on the hem of his shirt. He hesitates at first, like he's not sure he wants me taking it off. Then he relents.

"God," he growls as he helps me drag it off over his head. I rake my hands down his chest, which is springy with soft, cinnamon-colored hair. My gaze snags on a scar—a big one—just below his left shoulder. Before I can ask about it, he's tugging off my shirt.

"Chelsea." He says my name like a prayer as he tosses my shirt aside and lays me back on the bed to kiss his way down my torso.

Threading my fingers into his hair, I close my eyes and lose myself in the sensory explosion. My whole torso is a sheet of nerve endings, and he devours them all. Tongue, teeth, lips, beard—he uses everything to tease me to the brink of delirium. He's making love to me with his face, and he hasn't even gotten my pants off.

That happens next as he angles up and grips my waistband with both hands. He meets my eyes and I nod, and that's it. There's no need for words. He slides the leggings down my thighs and over my knees, and then I'm naked.

"Jesus Christ." His voice comes out strangled as he parts my thighs and looks at me. *Looks at me* like he's staring into a magical abyss or something. "You're so fucking beautiful."

I don't have a chance to make some self-conscious wisecrack.

He's on me in an instant, claiming me with his mouth. He devours me like he's starving, lapping at my swollen folds and moaning.

That feels good, too. The vibrations, the brush of his beard, the swirl of his tongue. I had no idea *not* having sex could feel this good.

He's got one hand cupping my hips but brings the other between my thighs. One long finger slips inside me, then slides back. I cry out, it feels so fucking good.

"Mark." I grip his head, afraid he'll take it as a cry of distress and stop. I don't want him to stop. I never want this to stop.

He takes his cue from the rising of my hips and keeps working his magic. There's thrusting and licking and swirling and sucking and somewhere in the middle of that I break apart.

"Oh, God!"

I scream like it's the first time I've felt this, and maybe it is. I've never come this hard before, and it's like a tidal wave of pleasure hitting me all at once. I clutch Mark's shoulders and throw my head back, riding the shockwaves until I'm breathless.

He waits until I go still to plant a kiss on my inner thigh. Then he slides up my body and pulls me against him. His bare chest is warm and the hair there is so soft. I run my fingers through it, still eager to touch him.

"Rest," he murmurs, turning me so my spine is cradled against his chest.

I can feel his erection pressing against my tailbone, and part of me aches to finish what we've started.

"Relax, Chelsea," he murmurs into my hair. "I've got you."

He does, so I let my body go slack in his arms.

The last thing I remember before drifting off to sleep is Mark brushing soft kisses down my earlobe.

CHAPTER 10

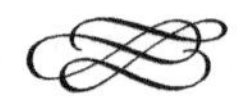

MARK

Austin calls early the next morning. "We've got some photos we'd like Chelsea to take a look at."

He must know I'm likely to be awake before the sun is up. Chelsea set an alarm for seven, and I try not to make noise as I nudge open her bedroom door to check on her.

She stirs and opens her eyes, and the smile that spreads across her face is like the sun coming out. "Hey." She sits up and pulls the sheet around her body, rumpled hair tumbling around her shoulders. "Good morning."

"Morning." God, she's fucking beautiful.

"Did you sleep at all?"

"Some." Not much. I couldn't bring myself to take my eyes off the front door for more than a few minutes.

Just those twenty minutes I spent in fucking nirvana with Chelsea's thighs around my face, my mouth on her—

"How'd you sleep?"

She must see something in my expression because her smile gets bigger, and she ignores the question. "Thank you for—everything," she says. "Last night."

The flush that spreads over her face and collarbones is a

good indication she's not talking about the bodyguard thing. I nod and fight the urge to push her back onto the bed so I can devour her again. "Austin's got some mugshots for you to look at."

That gets her moving. "You mean they got something off that fingerprint?" She's fully awake now, scrambling out of bed with the strap of her tank top slipping off one shoulder. I do my best not to stare at her breasts under the thin cotton or her ass in those tight little sleep shorts or her legs beneath—shit, I should just look at the floor.

"We should go right now," she says. "Before Libby comes home."

"I have a proposal."

There's a flash of alarm in her eyes, and I hurry to clarify so she doesn't think I'm dropping to one knee.

"For you and Libby," I tell her. "The resort has swimming pools."

She blinks, then seems to follow the subject change.

"I know, Libby loves it there," she says. "Bree let us come out last summer and test drive the waterslides. It was the highlight of Lib's life."

"So, we pack some clothes, lock up this place, and you two come have a vacation at Ponderosa Resort."

Chelsea tugs on a pink fluffy bathrobe, obscuring my view of her body, but allowing some blood to return to my brain. "I thought Bree told me the whole resort was booked for spring break."

"The resort is," I admit, hoping I'm not assuming too much here. "But my cabin has two master suites. For when my mom visits."

Her expression is guarded. "You don't have to put us up."

"I *want* to put you up," I argue. "I want you in a safe place with professional security. I want you to hike and get a massage and for Libby to swim in the pool and both of you to relax and not feel like you're watching out for someone trying to scare the shit out of you. Libby especially."

I have her there. I can tell from the flash of reluctant relief in her eyes. She wants her kid to be happy and cheerful and unaware that some asshole is trying to fuck with them.

"I did already plan to take the whole week off for Lib's spring break." She bites her lip. "Are you sure it's okay?"

"Positive."

She's still working that lip, and I'm overcome with the urge to claim her mouth again. "Get dressed," I tell her. "Or go shower. Do anything besides standing there looking like sex on a stick."

"Sex on a stick, huh?" She grins and tosses her hair. "That'd be a big seller at the bakery."

She turns and sashays toward the bathroom, and it's everything I can do not to follow her into the shower.

* * *

"THAT ONE," Chelsea says, pointing at a photo laid out on the desk in Austin's office.

Her hair is pulled back in a ponytail, and she's gripping a mug of coffee like it's a life preserver. She's pale and nervous, but determined. If I could, I'd cover her in bubble wrap to keep her safe from everything.

Austin's studying her face, and I can't tell what he's thinking. "Are you positive?"

"No." She sits back in her chair still gripping the mug. "Like I said, he wore a mask. His eyes were the only thing I could see, but that guy's look the same. Sort of a strange blue like pictures I've seen of icebergs."

Austin nods, frowning a little more than he was when we walked in here. "And you've never seen this man before yesterday?"

"No." Her ponytail sways as she shakes her head. "I'm sorry, I really think I'd remember him."

She's telling the truth, I'm positive. All along I've had the feeling she's holding something back, not filling in the full picture for Austin or me. But right now, she's being as truthful as she can be.

I stare at the photo she pointed to. The guy has weird blue eyes and a tattoo on his neck that might be a chicken. Or a rooster. What the hell kind of idiot inks poultry on the space between his face and body?

"Who is he?" I ask Austin. "The prints are his?"

Austin folds his hands on the desk and gives a curt nod. "Yes."

His expression is guarded, and I'm guessing Chelsea isn't the only one holding something back. "Name is Arthur Klingman," Austin supplies. "Goes by Artie. Small-time criminal, mostly burglary and petty theft."

"So, he tried to rob me." Chelsea says it halfway between a statement and a question, but I can tell she's not buying it. Not as the full story.

Neither is Austin. He clears his throat and leans back in his chair. "The thing about Artie is that he's a thief for hire," he says slowly. "He's not known for B and E without some motive. Without someone paying him for his time."

"You're saying someone hired him," I say slowly. "Who? And why?"

"I don't know." He looks pretty annoyed about that, and I'm betting he hates saying those words as much as I hate hearing them. "It's possible I'm wrong. Artie's got some charges for identity theft. Could be he was just looking to get his hands on credit cards or birth certificates or something."

He doesn't believe that, and I can see from Chelsea's face that she doesn't, either. She takes a long sip of her coffee like she's fortifying herself to ask the next question. "So now what?"

Austin nods at me. "I think Mark's got a solid idea about you staying out at the resort for a while," he says. "As far as Libby needs to know, this is just her spring break surprise."

Chelsea frowns. "What if he goes back? This Artie guy, what if he tries to get back into my house?"

"We'll be watching," Austin says. "We'll have a BOLO out on Arthur Klingman. He's not known for being the savviest criminal mastermind."

I wonder what else Austin's not saying. If he were a shitty cop, I'd wait for him to tell Bree, and then I'd badger her until she filled me in. But Austin's the best cop I know, so no member of the Bracelyn clan is going to get any details until he's damn good and ready.

Chelsea glances at her watch. "We have to go get Libby. Is there anything else I can tell you?"

"Nope." Austin unclasps his hands. "You're good to go. Thank you for coming in on such short notice."

"I wish I could do more." Chelsea stands, ponytail swinging over her shoulder as she pushes in her chair.

Austin stands, too, and I wonder if he's even scheduled to work today. It would be just like him to come in early on a day off. Call me crazy, but I don't think petty criminals are usually the domain of the police chief.

"We'll let you know if there's any news," he says. "Thank you for your help."

We say our goodbyes and head down the hall and out the door. We're halfway across the parking lot when Chelsea turns to me. "Would you mind driving?"

"No problem." I take the keys she's holding out and head around to the driver's side.

"Thanks," she says. "I got a text from the sleepover mom. Everyone's up now, so I'm going to see if we can swing by and get Libby instead of them dropping her at the house. That way we can go straight to your place."

"Good plan." I adjust the driver's seat while Chelsea taps out a message on her phone. I'm damn relieved we're not going back to her house. The sooner I get them both to the resort, the safer I'll feel.

"You doing okay?" I ask.

She doesn't answer right away. "I think so."

I shouldn't ask this next question, but I do anyway. "You're positive you have no idea what anyone would want from you? In your file cabinet or—"

"No."

No, she's not positive, or no, she has no idea? The curtness of the answer makes me think I shouldn't ask any more damn questions.

"I'm sorry, I'm just—" she hesitates, and I feel her eyes on the side of my head. "I need to think something through, okay?"

"Fair enough."

"Thank you." She's quiet for a few long minutes. "Really, Mark. I appreciate that you don't push. That you don't demand answers or information or things I'm not ready to talk about."

"Hey, I know all about not wanting to talk about shit."

"Yeah?"

"Yeah."

Which is how we end up not talking about any of it, even though I'm starting to think we ought to.

But Chelsea starts rattling off directions, and I drive us into a neat little subdivision on the west side of town. Libby comes running out before I've fully stopped the car at the curb, and she scrambles into the backseat with crooked pigtails and a waterfall of giggles. "We had waffles and fruit loops and Annabelle's kitten pooped on the floor."

She delivers this news with breathless enthusiasm as she buckles herself into her booster seat. If she's surprised to see me behind the wheel of her mom's car, she doesn't show it.

"...and we watched *Frozen* and ate popcorn, but Halie spilled some on the floor and then Emma peed the bed, but she tried to pretend it was Dipper." She finally takes a breath and looks at me in the rearview mirror. "Can we go see Long Long Peter?"

Chelsea's beside me in the passenger seat trying to look stern, but her eyes are filled with laughter. "Good morning to you, too, Miss Thing," she says. "Are you forgetting something? Like manners?"

"Oh." Libby grins at me. "Hi, Mark." She doesn't sound fazed, and her gap-toothed smile fills the rearview mirror as I pull away from the curb. "Can we go see Long Long Peter?"

"That's the plan," I tell her. "I hear you like swimming."

Her expression turns puzzled. "Rabbits can swim?"

Shit. I should probably take a class in communicating with children. Chelsea's rocking with laughter beside me, and I wonder if this is what it's like to have a kid in the house. No need for television when you've got this kind of entertainment.

"Peter's at my house," I tell her, deliberately omitting the first part of his name. "I live at Ponderosa Resort. Would you like to visit and go swimming?"

Her hazel eyes go wide. "We can go on the slides?"

"We can go on the slides," I confirm. "And afterward, we can get my brother to make us his famous chocolate banana strawberry waffles."

"Yes!" Libby bounces in her car seat, then launches into a rambling story that involves a Snickers bar, a broken hula hoop, cat litter, and a skateboard. The details are sort of fuzzy, but I admire the kid's enthusiasm.

Chelsea's smiling in the front seat, and somewhere between the edge of town and the road leading up to the resort, I get this warm, pinching feeling in my chest. Is this what it would be like to have a family of my own?

But no. That's crazytalk right there. How the hell could a guy with this many familial skeletons in his closet ever hope to have any sort of family of his own? That's not fair to anyone, especially Chelsea and Libby. God knows they've been through enough.

"Can we listen to music?" Libby asks from the backseat.

Chelsea frowns beside me. "Sorry, baby. I left my iPod back at the house."

"I have mine." Granted, I'm not sure what's on it, but I hand it over to Chelsea, and she hooks it up to her car's stereo system. "What did you have in mind?" I ask Libby.

"Maybe Mary Poppins soundtrack?"

"Um—" Yeah, I'm pretty sure that's not an option.

"Or how about Frozen?"

"How about Weird Al Yankovic?" I offer.

Libby's face screws up in confusion. "Who?"

Fortunately, Chelsea's quick with the iPod controls. She flips fast through my library, and the next thing I know, the three of us are singing along with "White and Nerdy."

Libby doesn't know the words, but she's giggling and humming and making up her own.

This.

A voice whispers the word in the back of my brain, and I fight to push it aside.

This is what you're missing.

No. I can't think like that. None of us can afford to.

I turn up the stereo volume and keep singing all the way to the resort.

Bree steps out onto my porch as I pull up in front of my cabin. I texted her the heads-up about bringing Chelsea and Libby home, so I shouldn't be surprised she's here pretending to perform some rabbit sitter duty as an excuse for sisterly nosiness.

"Hey, girls," she calls as Libby scrambles out of the car with Chelsea on her heels. "I hear you're in for a little spring break action."

"Yes!" Libby says as she flings her arms around Bree's legs before my sister can bend down to hug her properly. "We're having waffles in the swimming pool, and Mommy's sleeping with Mark, and I'm sleeping with Long Long Peter, and rabbits can't swim, but maybe Weird Owl Yankovic can."

Bree looks at me while she digests this news, the edges of her mouth tugging up. "Is that so?"

Chelsea gives Bree a pained look as my sister pulls her in for a hug. "I swear I said nothing to her about sleeping arrangements," she whispers as Libby scurries right through the front door like she owns the place. "You know how kids are."

"I do." Bree turns her smirk on me. "And I know my brother looks downright jolly this morning, so I'm going to go ahead and pat myself on the back for my matchmaking."

"Bite me," I mutter with absolutely zero venom.

Bree just laughs and yanks my arm so I'm forced to wrap my arms around her. "You get a hug, too, you big dummy. Thanks for being the hero last night."

"I'm no hero," I grumble, amazed as always by the fierceness of hugging from someone whose head only comes up to the middle of my chest. "Just a glorified babysitter."

She pulls back and looks at me. "If that's your idea of babysitting, remind me never to leave you in charge of my kids."

I scowl at her. "You're knocked up?"

"No." She smacks me in the arm. "My future kids. You'll be an uncle someday, you know."

The thought jars me, though I don't know why. It's not like it's never occurred to me my sister might breed. Or any of them, eventually. Sean and Amber are getting married, and isn't that what people do afterward?

"Hello? Earth to Mark?" Bree waves a hand in front of my face, and I look down at her. "You okay?"

"Yeah." I glance through my open front door and see Chelsea cradling Long Long Peter in her arms while Libby strokes his ears. They're well out of earshot, but I lower my voice anyway. "You ever wonder about how many of us there are?"

Bree frowns. "Is this some kind of philosophical discussion

about life on other planets? Because it's a little early in the morning for that."

"No, I mean *us*. Bracelyn kids. Dad got around. What if there's more kids? Or what if some of us are—"

Not his. Just say it. Spit it out.

"Bastards?" Bree touches my arm. "Is that what this is about?"

I stare at her, not sure how to respond. And pretty sure "bastard" isn't a word Libby needs to hear, though she's safely in the house with her face buried in rabbit fur.

"I was thinking about that this morning," Bree says, jerking me back to the conversation. "I was talking to your mom—"

"Since when do you talk with my mom?"

Bree sighs and ignores me. "I was talking to your mom and started wondering if it's ever weird for you that she and Dad never got married."

"It's not." What's weird is Bree talking to my mother, since my mom's the one Dad left Bree's mother for. Not that we ever talk about it because we're Bracelyns, and Bracelyns don't talk about stuff. It's in the handbook.

But seriously—what the hell?

Bree's still talking, and I'm trying to follow along. "You know none of us think less of you, right? That you're still exactly the same as the rest of us."

But I'm not. She has to know that, right?

She's staring at me like she's waiting for some kind of answer, but I don't know what to say.

Bree slugs me in the arm. "Don't make this weird. You know your mom and I talk sometimes."

A thread of gratitude winds its way around my heart as I realize she's totally missed why I've clammed up all of a sudden. She thinks it's about her relationship with my mother, which has always been...interesting.

"Your mom's a bitch," I mutter, and Bree nods in agreement. "You can borrow mine anytime."

"Thanks."

The lump in my throat isn't easing up, and I force myself to breathe. Is that what I spent my whole life doing with Cort Bracelyn? Borrowing a dad, pretending someone else's father was my own?

If that's true, who am I?

Not a brother, not to Bree or Sean or James or Jonathan or any of the other Bracelyn bastards running around out there.

And if that's the case, what right do I have to even be here? To spend this money, to live here at this resort like I have a place at the table with the rest of them.

Is that what James was getting at the other night?

"Mark?" Bree gives my arm a little shake. "You okay, big guy?"

"Yeah." I clear my throat. "Better get inside."

I trudge past her through the door, conscious of her eyes following me inside.

* * *

WE LITERALLY HAVE to drag Libby out of the pool to go eat brunch. I'm pretty sure it's lost on the kid that she's got a world-famous chef not only preparing her chocolate banana waffle, but hand-delivering it to her at our corner table.

"Whipped cream?" Sean asks, and Libby nods with a reverence that's almost holy.

"Yes," she breathes, then amends it when Chelsea shoots him a look. "Yes, please."

"Atta girl." Sean sets a bowl of sliced strawberries next to her, along with a bowl of his famous homemade applesauce. "Gotta make sure you get your vitamins." He winks at Chelsea. "I use whole wheat flour in the waffles, plus some other good stuff to make sure there's some nutritional value in there."

"Thank you," Chelsea says as Libby picks up her fork.

"Yes, thank you," Libby echoes as Sean sets an omelet in front of Chelsea with a flourish.

"Egg white omelet with fresh spinach, asparagus, caramelized shallots, gruyere, and cold-smoked Pacific Northwest salmon," he says. "The home-fried potatoes were sourced from a farm just down the road."

"Wow." Chelsea picks up her fork. "This looks amazing. Thank you."

"Bon Appetit."

Sean comes around to my side of the table and hands me my own stack of waffles, plus a pile of bacon, a side of home-fries smothered in gravy, and a bowl of the chocolate-dipped strawberries he knows I'm nuts about. "Don't say I never did anything for you."

"Hell, no," I say as I pick up my fork.

Shit, I'm not supposed to say *hell* in front of a kid. Or *shit.*

I mean, I didn't actually *say* shit, but isn't it wrong to think it in front of a kid? I didn't get the manual.

"Heck, no," I amend as Chelsea reaches over to help Libby cut up her waffle. "Thanks, man."

Sean nods. "No sweat." He stands there waiting for everyone to take a bite, which Chelsea does with an accompanying moan of pleasure.

"This is amazing, Sean," she says. "You're totally in the running for brother of the year."

Libby looks up in confusion. "Who's your brother?"

"They're brothers." Chelsea points to Sean and me, and Libby's gaze swings back and forth like her mom's just told her we're professional ballerinas.

"They don't look like brothers." She looks us up and down with the critical eye of a six-year-old, and I can't say I blame her.

"Families come in all shapes and sizes," Chelsea says, so fucking good at using everything as a teaching moment.

I kick myself for thinking the word *fucking* with a kid at the table while Chelsea continues with the lesson "And people don't all look the same," she says. "You know your friends Kate and Julia?"

Libby nods as a flicker of understanding passes over her freckled face. "They grew in China instead of in their mom's tummy, so they don't look like her, and they have a lizard named Marcel."

These details all make sense in a six-year-old way, so I nod like I'm part of this important life lesson. "Yeah," I add. "Sean and I don't have the same mom, but our dad—"

I stop there, unsure of a kid-friendly way to explain that our dad was a philandering cad.

"Dad spread a lot of love around," Sean supplies, which makes him sound like he organized orgies for a living.

I shouldn't think the word *orgy* around kids, either.

"He was a funny guy, our dad," I offer.

Libby's forehead gets all scrunchy. "Funny like Minions?"

"Sure," I say, not positive what Minions means, but pretty certain that's better than saying "funny like he stuck his dick in anything that moved."

I shouldn't think the word *dick* next to a kid.

"Sean, this is so good," Chelsea says as she chews a bite of Libby's waffle. "I'm already missing my bakery."

"Hey, you can help yourself to our pastry kitchen anytime."

"Pastry kitchen?" Chelsea's eyes light up. "You have a dedicated pastry kitchen?"

"Yep, and it's hardly ever used." Sean shrugs. "We're sorta between pastry chefs right now, so it's all yours if you want to play."

I nod at the key card sitting next to her plate, the one I programmed for all the resort facilities she might want to access. "I'll get that set up so you can go in there anytime," I tell her. "It's gotta be better than the bare bones oven at my place."

"It is," Sean agrees, stepping back from the table. "I need to get back to the kitchen." He slugs me in the shoulder. "See you at poker night."

"Thanks, Sean," Chelsea calls after him. "I promise to repay you with cupcakes for life."

I dive into my waffle, figuring I'm less likely to blurt out inappropriate kid shit if I keep my mouth full of food.

"Where is your dad?" Libby asks.

"Dead." I glance at Chelsea, who looks startled. "Passed away," I amend, wondering if that's the better word choice. "Pushing up daisies?" There, that sounds friendly.

Libby stabs her fork into a strawberry. "I don't have a dad."

I glance at Chelsea, not sure how to respond to that. She's not looking at me, intent on carving up her omelet into tiny little bites. "Libby, do you want to go back to the pool after lunch, or would you rather go on a bike ride?"

Libby screws up her face and thinks about that, paternity issues forgotten for the moment. "Bikes," she says. "Then swimming. Then rabbit. Then cake."

"Sounds like a plan," I tell her.

I've just shoved another bite of waffle into my face when James strides over. His shirt sleeves are rolled up, but his tie looks like he just ironed it. His hair is a little rumpled, but that's the extent of weekend casual for James.

"Sorry to bother you, but I've got a maintenance question." Noticing I'm not alone, he nods to Chelsea and Libby. "Ladies. Good afternoon."

Everyone chirps their greetings while I swipe at my beard with a napkin. "What's up?"

"Senator Grassnab's campaign launch party next week," he says. "They were planning to do it in the Liberty Ballroom, but RSVP numbers are coming in higher than they thought. His wife wants to know if we can move it outside."

"To the south lawn?"

"No, the bigger one. The one by the golf course. Is that a

problem with the PA system and the lawn maintenance stuff you were doing?"

"Nah." I take a slug of chocolate milk. "You checked the weather?"

"Yes," he says. "Zero chance of rain. Not that it rains a whole lot out in the high desert, but we're not expecting any spring thunderstorms."

I nod and consider how much time I'll need to spend on electrical to get us set up for an outdoor event that size. "We'll need space heaters if it's running into the evening," I tell him. "But we should be able to pull it off. Tell the senator sure."

"Perfect," James says. "Thanks for making it happen."

"If it makes you feel better, charge him extra for the hassle."

James snorts. "An Oregon senator announcing his run for president, and he's doing it here," James says. "I'm half tempted to give it to him for free, just for the publicity this buys us."

"Do what you've gotta do," I tell him.

I turn back to Libby and Chelsea, thinking I ought to say something about brothers or jobs or the U.S. political system. Some kind of age-appropriate teaching moment.

That's when I notice Chelsea's gone white as a pile of powdered sugar. "You okay?"

She nods and flashes a smile that looks glued on. "Fine. Totally. I just—I thought maybe I left the oven on."

"At your house?"

She nods, but the color isn't returning to her face. "It's probably nothing. Just being paranoid."

This time, her smile almost reaches her eyes. She turns to Libby and busies herself cutting slices of waffle, slicing it into bite-sized pieces. I watch for a second, wondering what the hell I just missed.

Glancing back at James, I shoot him a "what the hell?" look.

But since James is even more clueless than I am, he hasn't noticed a damn thing. "Will I see you at poker night?"

"Sure," James says with as much enthusiasm as if I'd invited him to a biker brawl. "Your place, right?"

"Six-thirty," I tell him. "Don't be late."

"I never am."

He wanders away and I glance back at Libby and Chelsea. They're talking and laughing and trading bites of food, and I think maybe I imagined the whole thing a few minutes ago.

Or did I?

CHAPTER 11

CHELSEA

"You're positive this is okay?" I study Mark's face, looking for any sign he's freaking out.

"Go," he says. "I've got this."

The sexiest three words a man can say, but still, I'm nervous. We're standing in the doorway of his cabin with the earthy spring breeze wafting in off the pond. The sun is almost down for the count, but it's spurting little bursts of red and orange as it disappears behind the mountains.

I turn back to Mark, who's radiating vibes as the world's foremost lumberjack nanny. The fact that he's cradling a rabbit in his arms completes the picture.

"It's a lot to ask," I tell him as I scratch Long Long Peter behind his velvety ears. "You've barely just met Libby, and you said yourself you haven't been around kids much. You're sure this is okay for two whole hours?"

He adjusts the rabbit in his arms, and I'm momentarily distracted by the size of his biceps. By the memory of having them envelop me completely.

"Two hours in which she'll be fast asleep the whole time," he reminds me. "Besides, I'm not flying solo. I'll have a cop, a chef, a doctor, a lawyer, an international humanitarian, and a U.S. Marine whose seasonal gig is playing Santa. I think we can figure out how to pour her a glass of water if she wakes up."

When he puts it that way, I feel silly for worrying.

But I also feel guilty for going out for a girls' spa night when someone may or may not be trying to harm me. "If someone's out to get me, should I really be off getting a Moor peat bath?"

"What's a meat bath?"

Apparently, he hasn't spent two hours studying the spa services menu like I did today. "I don't know what it is, either," I admit. "It's been a while since I had any sort of spa date."

"Which is why you should go and not worry."

I bite my lip and glance out over the resort grounds. The towering wood buildings are bathed in sunset hues of pink and gold, and the golf course sprawls on the horizon like a sheet of green velvet. Coyote song and juniper breeze swirl together to create the most perfect blend of sound and smell, and it's so beautiful here I want to lie down in the grass and just soak it all in.

"The place is crawling with private security," Mark says, misreading my sigh. "We've always got it, but there's even more with the senator coming this week. You're safe, I promise."

Goosebumps ripple up my arms. They've got nothing to do with the sage-laced breeze that just shivered past. "Thank you." I turn back to smile at him. "I trust you."

Something flickers in his eyes. I can't quite read it, but it's gone as fast as it appeared. "You kissed her goodnight already?" he asks. "Made sure she's asleep and everything?"

"Yes." I bite my lip. "I owe you, Mark."

"You don't owe me jack." He shifts Long Long Peter to the crook of his elbow and puts a hand on my back to usher me along. "Go. Poker night starts in ten minutes. You can't be here; it's the rule."

"Thank you." I stand up on tippy toe to kiss him. It's supposed to be a chaste kiss, but somehow it lands closer to his mouth and ends up lasting a good ten seconds.

Only the rabbit wiggling between us forces us to break apart. When we draw back, he looks as mind-whacked as I feel.

"Fuck." He rakes a hand through his hair and shakes his head. "How do you do that?"

"Do what?" I'm honestly not sure what he means.

"Leave me feeling like I washed down two pounds of gummy bears with a bottle of champagne." He frowns, probably replaying those words in his head. "That sounded weirder than I meant it to."

"I feel the same." I do, even though I wouldn't have used quite those same words. But I know I need to go if I want to make it to spa night instead of ending up wrapped around his body like a koala hugging a tree.

I take a step back. "Thanks again." My voice is breathless, and I'm ten seconds from saying to hell with spa night and begging him to take me to bed.

But no, he's got half the town's men on their way here right now. And I've got half the women waiting for me

"Have fun," he calls from the front porch as I make my way across the paved trail toward the spa.

Twilight has dropped like a curtain while we've been talking, but the full moon lights my way even better than the hammered copper light fixtures lining the path. I breathe in all my favorite springtime smells—bitterbrush, the oven-baked spice of ponderosa bark, and whatever Sean's cooking up at the lodge. The whole mix is mouthwatering.

The grass squishes under my shoes when I step off the path, but it hasn't rained. Must be the irrigation, which I know Mark tweaked earlier today to get ready for the senator's visit.

I shiver and pull my sweater tighter around me, hustling to reach the spa. I climb the pebble-speckled steps to the massive rippled-glass doors marking the entry. They're supposed to look like water, and I hear it bubbling around me from the man-made creek meandering through the courtyard.

They spared no expense with this place.

Pushing through the doors, I nearly collide with Bree. She's scurrying across the lobby with a bottle of champagne in each hand, and she breaks into a big grin when she sees me. "Chelsea, you made it!" She sweeps me in to a hug, bumping my back with the bottles. Her dark curls are swept into a loose topknot, and she smells like lavender and sunshine.

"Come on," she says, drawing back and looping her arm through mine. "Let's get you inside."

"You're sure this is okay?" I fall into step beside her, feeling oddly guilty about accepting an all-expenses paid girls' spa night. "I don't want to take advantage."

"Please," Bree scoffs, leading the way down a lavender-scented hallway lined with sconces that drizzle warm, golden light down the sage-hued walls. "We had a whole bridal party cancel at the last second, but it was too late to call off the extra spa staff. You're doing us a favor."

I make a mental note to tip well tonight, even though I'm positive Bree's got it covered. More than covered. The Bracelyns are known for generosity with their staff. "Am I benefitting from someone else's misfortune?"

"You mean the bridal party that cancelled?" Bree snorts as we approach a rustic wood door with flashy copper inlays. "You're benefitting from the fact that the groom couldn't keep it in his pants."

Yikes. "Seems like the bridal party would really need the spa night after something like that."

"Oh, they're getting it." Bree grins and pushes through the door. "The bride's flying all her friends and family to Jamaica on the ex-groom's dime. I already sent flowers to her suite."

And this is how the other half lives.

I follow Bree into a room done in dusty pastels and plush

white furniture. Harp music trickles from hidden speakers in the walls, and the air swirls with lemongrass and female laughter.

Everyone looks up as we enter, and I recognize a sea of familiar faces.

"Chelsea!" Amber King waves me over to the chaise lounge where she's perched next to Lily Archer. "Welcome to the relaxation suite. Feeling relaxed yet?"

"Here, this will help." Lily slips a champagne flute into my hand. "Mimosas. Yum."

"This is all so exotic." I survey the blissed-out ladies chattering around me and realize I'm the only one not wearing a plush white robe. Was I supposed to bring one? "I've only been to a spa once in my life, and that was a prenatal thing my mom bought me on a Groupon."

I was eight months pregnant at the time and spent the whole sixty minutes having to pee so badly I couldn't relax.

"Word of advice." Lily leans in conspiratorially, and I find myself moving closer. "Don't ask for a happy ending massage. Apparently, they don't do that in a classy place like this."

"You did *not* ask for that." Amber elbows her in the ribs, and I remember they played soccer together in high school. Their teasing repartee is as familiar to me as the spiced scent of Lily's perfume.

"Tramp," Amber declares good-naturedly.

"Hussy," counters Lily, smirking.

I'm eighty-five percent sure they're kidding about the happy ending, but you never know with Lily. She wears her sexuality like a badge of honor, something I've always kinda admired.

"Floozy," Amber counters.

"Jezebel."

"Trollop."

I take a sip of my mimosa, enjoying the show. Bree is going around topping off glasses and reminding people to fill out forms specifying the type of massage they like and what sort of facial services they want. I did mine online already, taking wild guesses about what parafango and effleurage meant. Either I ordered a massage or a sandwich.

"Hey, Chelsea." I turn to see Jade King striding into the room in jeans and sock feet. She's carrying her work boots, which are caked with mud. It's entirely possible she drove a tractor here.

"Good, I'm not the only one who's late," she says. "Come on, let's grab robes."

I follow her around a corner and through another doorway, grateful she's been here before. Must be a perk of marrying into this family. "How's Brandon?" I ask.

"Great." Her whole face lights up at the mention of her fiancé. Tossing her caramel-colored ponytail, she shrugs off her flannel overshirt and grabs the hem of her pink tee. "He's playing cards with your guy, right?"

My guy. Is that who Mark is? She must see my hesitation because she makes a face. "Sorry, I wasn't trying to be nosy."

Jade whips off her T-shirt with an unselfconsciousness I envy. We were a few years apart in school, but I know she was teased for being a chubby kid. Jade got the last laugh, growing up to be a beautiful, badass reindeer rancher who could probably bench press her former tormentors while wearing high heels and a kickass dress.

Not that she wears anything but jeans most of the time. She wriggles out of hers and the stretch marks on her hips make me instantly less self-conscious about my own.

"Small town life," I say, stripping off my own T-shirt. "I figure we all sort of know each other's business, right?"

"Right." She kicks off her jeans and starts shoving things into a locker behind her. "You've had some scary stuff happening."

I recognize the statement for what it is. Not nosiness, but an invitation to talk if I need a shoulder.

For the millionth time, I wonder how much she knows. How much they all know. The single mom thing earns me a certain amount of privacy, but I'm not dumb enough to think people don't gossip. What has Jade heard?

"It's been a little scary," I admit as I fold my shirt and jeans into a locker. "I could have blown off the smaller stuff—the hang-up calls, even the vandalism. But having someone break into my house—"

"It's creepy, isn't it?"

That's right, I forgot. Jade and Amber had some problems out at the ranch the Christmas they opened. She knows better than most what it's like to feel unsafe in your own home.

"I'm trying to keep things as normal as possible for Libby," I say, which isn't exactly an answer to her question.

"She's doing okay?" Jade's stripping off her skivvies, and I'm glad I've got her here to show me what to do. I'd have no clue.

"Lib's good," I say as I peel off my polka-dotted bra and panties and wonder if she knows I bought them with Mark in mind. "Right now, she just thinks we're on vacation."

"Give me a call if you want to bring her out to see the reindeer," Jade offers. "That's a good distraction."

"I might take you up on that."

Jade pulls two fluffy white robes off a rack behind her. She offers one to me, then shrugs into her own. "Let me know if you need anything else. A home-cooked meal. Someone to watch Libby. A team of Marines sent out to beat someone up."

I laugh, appreciating the support. "Mark might appreciate the backup troops."

There's his name again, hovering in the air between us like a flirty UFO. Jade watches my face, trying to figure out if that's my awkward way of admitting I kinda want to talk about him.

"I've always liked Mark," she says. "He's so gruff on the outside, but he's really just a great big marshmallow."

"That's what I love about him."

Love? Did I just say that?

Jade's trying not to react, but I can see her noticing.

"I didn't mean—we're not—I mean—"

"It's okay." She offers an encouraging smile. "I know you like to keep things private."

There's a long pause, and she's watching me like she's waiting for something else. "You know," she says slowly, "If you ever need to talk about anything, you can count on me to be discreet."

"I know."

Her blue eyes are clear, and she holds mine with such intense kindness that I can't look away. "I know what it's like to hold things in," she says. "Stuff you think you can't talk about, so you bottle it up tight. Just know you can come to me anytime if you need to unburden."

I hold my breath, wondering what she knows. What any of them know. I've been so careful, so guarded about everything.

But if Jade knows, that means other people could know, and that means—

"Thank you," I say. "I'll let you know."

"Come on." Jade grins as I cinch up the belt on my robe. "Let's go have some hot guys rub us."

CHAPTER 12

MARK

"This is the weirdest guys' night I've ever been to." Brandon Brown reaches across the table for the carton of chocolate milk and pours some into his glass. "Really fucking strange."

"Shut the fu—fudge up," I tell him. "You can't swear with a kid in the house."

The rest of the guys have the good sense not to respond. They're too busy shuffling their cards and eating the cupcakes I set out for them on a plate in the middle of the table.

All right, maybe I've gone overboard. It's the first time I've been left in charge of a kid, so I didn't feel right cracking beers and putting some violent-ass hockey game on TV.

"Is there seriously not anything else we can watch?" Sean grumbles. He reaches across me to grab a hunk of salami off the charcuterie tray he brought, and I'm grateful I invited a chef. If it weren't for him, we'd have nothing but sweets to snack on.

Brandon frowns at the TV as he shuffles his cards. "What are we watching, anyway?"

"Yo Gabba Gabba." Dr. Bradley Parker shuffles his cards on the other side of the table. "Watched a lot of this when I did my pediatrics residency. This is the one where they sing *Party in My Tummy*."

"Excellent," Sean mutters. "Now I know the theme for that bridal luncheon I have to do next week."

Dr. Parker—I should probably just call him Bradley—laughs and studies his cards. He's new to the group, hired on recently at one of the local clinics. I haven't talked to him much, what with all the worrying about Libby and Chelsea, but Austin says he's a good guy.

"Look on the bright side," Austin points out as he helps himself to a pomegranate buttercream cupcake. "At least we get to play poker and not pattycake."

James is standing by the fireplace scowling at his phone, having already folded for this hand. He looks up long enough to frown at something else on the other side of my couch. "Is that animal supposed to be shitting in that box?"

"Don't say shitting," I tell him. "It's a rabbit. And that's his litterbox."

And this is my life. How the hell did that happen?

I should probably feel weird about it, but I just feel—happy?

Sean snorts beside me. "Ask Mark what his rabbit's name is."

I glare at my brother. "Ask Sean how old he was before he stopped wetting the bed."

I have no idea if that's true, since Sean and I grew up on opposite sides of the country with mothers who couldn't have been more different if they'd tried. But he shuts up anyway, and I wonder if I'm getting the hang of this brother thing. Maybe my fake-it-'til-I-make-it strategy is working.

"Whaddya got, bro?" Sean throws some poker chips into the middle of the table and lays his cards down. "I'm calling you."

Well damn. I sigh and toss my cards down.

"I've got Jack shi—shart," I admit, spreading out my cards to display the lousiest hand I've had the whole game.

Normally, this is where I'd cheerfully invite him to go fuck himself in the spirit of friendly poker play, but instead I say "nice job."

See? I'm catching on.

"Ha!" Sean scrapes the chips toward him, looking downright cheerful. "I knew you were bluffing. You're a shitty liar."

"Don't say shitty," I grumble, ignoring the rest of the insult. Sean knows better than some what it's like to hide a secret. He spent the better part of his life covering a pretty big one for his mom. What would he think if he knew about mine?

"Gotta say, I always wanted this." Jonathan hoists his glass of chocolate milk in a toast. "Brotherly poker games, belching and farting, all the guy stuff I never got. Maybe I'll move out here with the rest of you bast—bastions of brotherly love."

A lump forms in my throat, and it's not because I feel sorry for Jonathan being raised with six half-sisters. It's the look he just exchanged with James, a look that says the two of them know something I don't. I turn toward Sean in time to see him glance away fast.

What the hell?

Before my paranoia can take over, Austin's phone buzzes. He and Doc Parker are the only two not banned from having phones at the poker table, and he frowns as he looks at the screen. "Deal me out, please."

He stands up and strides fast into the kitchen, and I wonder if it has anything to do with Chelsea. That's probably wishful thinking on my part. I want them to nail the bastard who's been turning her life upside down, who's scaring an innocent six-year-old for no good reason.

I know I shouldn't, but I watch Austin's face as he talks, trying to read his lips. Was that *Charlie* he just said? Not like I can read lips, so it could be anything.

"Hey, kiddo, what are you doing up?"

I whip around to see Sean peering down the hallway. In the time it takes for Libby to emerge, I do a fast rewind through the last two minutes of conversation. Pretty sure none of us have said anything too shitty.

Libby trudges sleepily into the room wearing a pair of fuzzy pink pants and a white shirt with cartoon pictures of ducks. Her feet are bare, her hair is rumpled, and she looks so damn adorable my heart gives a painful squeeze.

She does a bleary blink at the table full of men, taking inventory of the strangers before her gaze lands on me. Her face brightens, and she scurries forward, rubbing her eyes.

"I had a dream." She clambers onto my lap like she belongs there, and my arms go around her by instinct, like they're thinking the same damn thing.

"A dream, huh?"

She nods, blessedly unworried by the roomful of strange men she's never seen before. "I was eating clouds because they tasted like cotton candy," she continues, snuggling against my chest. "And then a dog came and peed on them, and I was sad so I cried, and now I need grape soda."

Well, shit. I can't argue with that logic.

Or can I?

"I don't think you're supposed to have sugar after bedtime," I say, pretty sure that's right. "How about some water?"

"Okay."

Sean jumps up to go get it, and I nod my thanks as Lib keeps talking. "The bed is really soft, but it would be softer if Long Long Peter slept with me."

Also, true, and also not a great idea. Maybe my kid instincts aren't so bad.

"How about another blanket?" I offer. "I've got a fuzzy red one my mom gave me when I moved in here. She said everyone who owns a mountain cabin needs a fuzzy blanket."

"Your mom sounds nice," she says. "Where's my mom?"

She sounds more curious than worried, but I keep my voice

gentle anyway. "She's having fun with her friends," I tell her. "Like I'm having fun with my friends."

Libby surveys the assembled men, most of whom are studying her like she's some kind of zoo animal. No, that's me. They're looking at *me* like this is the oddest thing they've seen all week.

"Looks good on you," Jonathan murmurs, meeting my eyes.

Over by the fireplace, James nods. "You're a natural."

I try to think of some smartass answer, but I don't want to get Libby asking questions. She squirms in my lap to look up at me, her hazel eyes nearly melting my heart. "Sing to me?"

"Sing?"

I say it like she's just asked me to stand up on the table and punch myself in the nuts, and I do my best to backtrack. "Uh, I don't really know any—"

"Yeah, *sing*." Sean grins, getting me back for that bedwetting joke. "What's that one you taught me that one summer we were out here together?"

Shit, he's right. There was one summer we wound up visiting Dad at the same time. I was ten, and Sean was maybe eleven, on break from some fancy summer camp. James was there, too, and they both kept yammering on about shit they'd learned at boarding school. I wasn't jealous, exactly. I just didn't have much to contribute except some dirty jokes and a few goofy songs I'd learned at school.

"Something about humps," Sean prompts, and I start to stand so I can punch him.

But Libby claps her hands together and bounces. "Alice the Camel. That's my favorite song."

No shit? "Um, wow." I scrub a hand over my beard. "I'm not sure I remember how—"

"Alice the Camel has—" Lib claps, her small hands smacking together with surprising force. "Ten humps!"

It's coming back to me now, this silly childhood tune that seems ridiculous now. As a ten-year-old, I probably just liked the excuse to say "hump" without my mom washing my mouth out with soap.

Libby's still going, and apparently, so is the damned camel.

"...so go, Alice, goooo," she hoots, really getting into it now. "Alice the camel has—" She stretches up and claps the sides of my face with both hands, shouting the words up into my face. "Nine humps!"

I can't help it. The kid's energy is contagious, and so is her joy over this ridiculous song.

"Alice the camel has—" I clap my hands, muscle memory taking me back to the edge of the pond where I taught this to Sean and James so many years ago. They were older than me and laughed their asses off, but I didn't care. I was so fucking happy to know something they didn't, even if it was some lame-ass kids' song.

"—Nine humps."

A pang of guilt hits me about shouting "hump" in front of a kid, but I think it's okay in this context. Lib's having a ball, clapping and singing and smacking her hands in my beard every time she gets to another hump.

The other guys start getting into it, too, whacking their hands on the table and joining the singalong. They're all wearing dorky grins, and I remember what Brandon said about this being the weirdest guys' night in history. But he doesn't seem to mind as he claps and joins the next verse.

"Alice the camel has—" *clap!* "—six humps."

Even James loosens his tie and starts nodding his head in time to our tuneless melody. Austin's taken his phone conversation outside, and I realize I'd forgotten about all of it. The bad guys, the bloodlines, all the reasons I've told myself I couldn't have a wife and family.

In that moment, I almost think I could do it.

"Alice the camel has—" *clap!* "—no humps, so nooow Alice is a horse!"

All of us finish in a shouted chorus of voices I'm sure they can hear down at the lodge. There's even a last-second tenor harmony thrown in that I'm pretty sure is James, even though he's not moving his lips.

When the last note fades, Libby claps her hands together and squeals. "You have to come to my birthday party and sing."

"Um," I say, regrouping. "When's your birthday party?"

"June five," she reports matter-of-factly.

And just like that, the lump is back in my throat. *June fifth.* That's almost three months away.

I'm back in my childhood bedroom, the evening of my eighth birthday. The covers are pulled up to my ears, even though it's still light outside, and my mother wears a worried look as she comes in to check on me.

"How are you, baby?" She sits on the side of my bed, stroking my hair while I pretend not to cry.

"He said he'd be here," I sniffle, rubbing my cheek against the soft flannel of my pillowcase. "He said he'd come to my party."

"I know he did, sweetheart," she soothes, her voice comforting but not surprised. Not by that point. "Sometimes men are disappointing. Women, too," she adds quickly as an afterthought, but I know she doesn't mean it.

Men are the ones who leave people crying. I know that even then.

"My dad promised," I sniffle, hating myself for crying because I damn sure couldn't hate him. "Is he not coming because of Joe?"

Joe, that was his name. I'd almost forgotten. My mother's boyfriend at the time, one of several she had over the years. That was another conversation I'd eavesdropped on, knowing damn well I wasn't supposed to hear.

"I'm not coming if your damn boyfriend's going to be there," my father muttered, pacing in the living room of the small house I shared with my mom.

"That's your choice, Cort." My mom was using her calm voice, the one she used with her pre-school students. "But I want you to think very hard about how Mark is going to feel."

"Think about how *I* feel," my father snapped. "How many times do I have to ask you to marry me before you'll—"

"—ignore my own wishes and give in to yours?" My mom made a tsk sound I recognized from the last time I'd tried to convince her to serve cookies for dinner. "I love you, Cort. I'll always love you on some level, and I appreciate that you take care of us. But we both know you'll never be faithful, and I deserve more than that."

My father muttered some more choice curses, but even then, I knew my mom was right.

That didn't make it any easier to have both men—my dad and Joe—fail to show for my party.

I know it's stupid. I know my fragile, eight-year-old heart should have healed by now, but it wasn't about the birthday party. It was learning dads could come and go. That mine could vanish in an instant, snatching away everything I believed about my father, about my family, about myself.

Blinking back the memories, I realize Libby's still looking at me. Her hazel eyes are wide as she waits for an answer.

"Your birthday's a long ways off," I tell her, dodging the question like the asshole I am. "A lot can change by then."

"Not family," she says. "Family doesn't change."

I can't breathe. I can speak or blink or even swallow. It's like my whole body is paralyzed, and I don't know what to do.

It's Doc Bradley who notices, probably realizing I'm on the brink of some medical meltdown. He stands up and shuffles toward the kitchen, even though it's the first time he's set foot in my house. "Who wants more chocolate milk?" he asks.

Libby tears her eyes off me and gives a little squeak of joy. "Yes, please."

The birthday invitation is forgotten for now, at least by Libby.

Not by the asshole who can't even answer a kid's innocent question with anything other than bullshit.

"I'll take some more," I mumble, nodding my thanks to the doc.

Sean stands up, too, ready to refresh his charcuterie tray, but mostly to escape the awkwardness of the moment. Or maybe that's my imagination, because he puts a hand on my shoulder and squeezes when he walks past.

I'm still wondering if I should say something to Libby about the birthday thing when Austin walks back into the room. He looks at me, and I can tell something's wrong. I lift an eyebrow, and he shakes his head. It's a wordless conversation that translates roughly as "What the fuck?" and "Not now."

On my lap, Libby yawns. She tries to cover it, but I scoop her into my arms and stand. "Pretty sure you're supposed to be in bed," I tell her.

"But my chocolate milk—"

"I'll bring it to you in just a minute," I assure her as I carry her down the hall to the guest room.

I start to tap the light switch with my elbow, then notice Chelsea plugged some kind of nightlight thing into the outlet beside the bed. The mom-ness of the gesture is so sweet and thoughtful that my chest fills with the same warm glow pouring from the star-shaped light.

And then I feel like an asshole all over again, because I'd never in a million years think of bringing a nightlight. Or knowing what songs to sing. Or how not to leave a kid crying in six months if things don't work out between her mom and me.

"There you go," I tell Libby as I stuff her under the covers and do my best to tuck them up around her face. "Snug as a bug in a rug."

It's something my mom used to say to me, and it makes Libby giggle. "Can I have a story?"

"A story?" I fumble though my brain trying to remember one.

"Cinderella had this nasty stepmother and evil stepsisters and one day she went to a ball in a pumpkin and lost her shoe but kissed a prince and in the end they got married."

Libby blinks at me. "That was fast."

"Yeah."

"Maybe next time you could use a book?"

Next time? I love this kid's faith in me. Or in the world at large, as a thing that might not end up disappointing her. "Next time," I say, wondering if there will be one.

"Good night, Mark." She stretches her arms up straight, and for a second, I'm not sure what that's about.

A hug, dumbass.

I lean down to embrace her, breathing in the sweet scent of strawberry shampoo. God, what I wouldn't do to deserve the kind of unconditional affection this kid doles out like it's free. Like it's not the riskiest, scariest thing in the whole damn world.

"Good night." I breathe the words like a prayer, feeling her go slack in my arms like she's already drifting off to sleep.

When I draw back, her eyelids flutter closed like they're weighted by sandbags, and she sinks into that kind of heavy, effortless slumber you can only enjoy when you're six.

"Sweet dreams," I whisper, wishing it was really that simple.

CHAPTER 13

CHELSEA

Bree insists on walking me back to the cabin, even though I see no fewer than three security guards lining the well-lit pathway from the spa to Mark's place. I wonder if her choice to tag along has something to do with the text she got while we were finishing up our pedicures.

"God, this feels amazing." Bree rolls her head around on her neck, sighing with pleasure. "I don't know why I don't do the massage thing more often."

"It is pretty nice," I agree, breathing in huge lungfuls of fresh spring air. The night is crisp and fragrant, with a thick perfume of bitterbrush filling the air. A nighthawk swoops past, chirping its warning to stay the hell away from its babies. I can relate.

"Before I forget, Mark's birthday is Wednesday," she says.

"Really?" A ripple of embarrassment moves through me. Shouldn't a woman know the birthdate of a guy she's been intimate with? "He never mentioned it."

"Of course he didn't," Bree says, dodging sideways to avoid the spray of a sprinkler. "I'm only telling you because I knew he wouldn't, and I didn't want you to feel awkward when people start showing up to surprise him."

"People?" I glance at Bree, wondering just how many people we're talking about.

"Okay, don't tell, but we're planning a big surprise party," she says. "His mom's coming over from Portland, and we've hired a bluegrass band to play, and Sean's got this menu of all his favorite foods. It's going to be tons of fun, and I hope you can be there."

Wow. The Bracelyns go all out for birthdays. "Is it a milestone birthday or something?"

She looks at me oddly, and I feel like a total dumbass.

"He's turning thirty," she says. "I guess guys don't make a big deal of it the way women do. He probably thinks we've all forgotten. Knowing him, he wouldn't care at all."

"Yes, he would." The words slip out before I can stop them, and I'm as surprised as Bree. "He cares about you guys a lot more than he lets on. Family—it's really important to him."

She studies me for a moment, green eyes missing nothing. "You know, you're right," she says. "I take it for granted sometimes that we've settled into this ready-made family and started a business together. It's different for Mark than it is for me or Sean or James or the rest of us."

"How do you mean?"

Bree doesn't answer right away, and I appreciate that she's choosing her words carefully. "He grew up really close to his mom," she says. "The rest of us were packed off to boarding schools and were lucky if we saw our families on holidays. But Mark—he and his mom were tight. Did he tell you he saved her life?"

"What? No!" Should I know this already?

Bree shakes her head, murmuring softly to herself. "I'm not surprised. He's modest. There was a house fire. He came home to find the whole place up in flames. Ran inside and grabbed his mother, who'd already passed out from smoke inhalation—"

"Jesus."

"He was sixteen." Bree says nothing for a moment, letting that sink in. "His birthday, actually. He was coming home from school and—well, I actually don't know all the details."

And I knew none of them. Not a single one. "Sounds pretty scary."

Bree keeps walking, her eyes on the path in front of us. "He's never said a word about it to any of us. The only reason I know is that Dad told me. He changed the date of my visit that year because Mark had to stay in the hospital. I guess he got a pretty bad burn on his chest."

"That's what that's from?"

Bree stops walking and cocks her head at me. "Seen him shirtless, have you?"

Busted.

Wait, no. "We were at the pool together all afternoon."

"Sure, that's it." Bree smirks.

I turn my eyes back on the path ahead, grateful to the darkness for masking my flaming face. "We haven't slept together, if that's what you're thinking."

"I wasn't, but thanks for volunteering the info." She starts walking again. "Not that you need my approval, but you have it. If you're wondering if the family is cool with Mark dating you, the answer is a resounding 'hell yes.'"

"Great." My breath comes out in an unladylike snort. "Now we just need *his* approval."

"You think you don't have it?"

"I'm not sure." We're almost to the cabin now, and I slow my pace, not ready to end this conversation. "He's holding back. I don't know what it is exactly, but it makes me paranoid."

"Spoken like a woman who's been lied to before."

"Yep." I bite my lip. "Not that I think he's lying, exactly. Just—I don't know. Hiding something, maybe?"

"It's possible," Bree muses. "Bracelyns aren't known for being open and forthright." She glances at me, green eyes sparking with curiosity. "Any suspicions what it might be?"

I'm trying not to feel depressed by this conversation. Part of me wishes Bree were falling all over herself insisting her brother is a wide-open book. That he couldn't possibly be shutting me out.

But we both know that's not the case. "Maybe there's nothing," I say. "But I can't help thinking he's got some sort of hang-up about family."

Bree laughs and slings an arm around me. "You've met our family," she says. "It would be a shocker if any of us didn't have hang-ups related to that."

Her arm stays looped around my shoulders as we make our way up the steps. That's when I notice Austin's truck is still parked out front.

Bree doesn't knock. Just walks right in, which is either a courtesy to Libby sleeping or a sign that she's nosy as hell. Either way, I follow her inside, listening for the sound of male voices.

As we walk into the living room, I'm struck by a scene from the world's weirdest children's book. A uniformed police officer I've never seen before sits in the oversized leather chair with a rabbit stretched out across his knees.

Kitty-corner from him is Mark in lumberjack plaid. He's scrubbing a hand over his beard, looking pensive and edgy. He glances up as we walk in, and there's something I can't read in his brown eyes.

"Chelsea," he says. "Everything okay?"

I'm not sure if he's talking about the spa date or if something else happened, but I nod as I reach the living room. "Of course. What's going on?"

"Ma'am." The uniformed officer sets the rabbit on the floor and stands as Austin comes in from outside. Everyone turns to look at him as he strides across the room to join us.

"Chelsea." Austin nods at me, then stoops to give Bree a quick kiss. "Just taking a look outside. Mark thought he heard a noise."

"What kind of noise?" I glance at Mark, grateful his instincts told him to stay inside with Libby while an armed cop checked it out.

"Like something hitting the side of the house," he mutters. "Probably nothing. We're all getting a little paranoid."

Austin's still standing beside me, and he clears his throat. "Chelsea, have a seat," he says. "Officer Leopold here brought some photos for you to look at."

Mark scoots over to make room for me, and I settle in beside him. I study his face, wondering if I should be worried. "Is Libby—"

"Fast asleep," he says. "With the door closed and a cowbell hanging from the doorknob so we'll hear her coming if she steps out."

I have so many questions, not the least of which is where the hell did Mark get a cowbell? But Officer Leopold is spreading photos out on the coffee table, so I direct my attention at him.

"There are some more graphic ones in this envelope," he says. "But we'll start with these. Do you recognize this man?"

I stare at the photos. The guy in the photo has a scruffy blond beard and a scar across one cheek. He's about fifty pounds heavier than I remember, but I'd know that face anywhere.

"That's Charlie." I swallow hard, trying to get my bearings. "Charles Crawford, a guy I dated years ago."

Bree peers over my shoulder and frowns. "Something looks weird about him."

I glance back at the photos, and that's when I notice. His eyes are open, but he lies motionless looking still and stiff and—

"Dead?" I look up at the police, both of whom have lapsed into stoic cop mode. "Is he dead?"

"Yes, ma'am." Officer Leopold looks at Austin, then back at me. "He was shot three times at close range. In the—uh—groin area."

"Oh my God." I frown down at the photos, noticing they're all from the waist up. "What happened?"

"His wife," Austin says. "They'd only been married a few months, but he took her last name. Hiding his identity, probably. That's why we couldn't track him down right away."

I stare at the images, not sure what to say. This person I loved once is dead. I hated him more than I loved him, and feared him even more than that, but still. That's a lot of emotion to have tangled up with someone whose pulse isn't beating anymore.

Mark must sense my mixed-up stew of emotions because he reaches over and puts a steadying hand over mine. "Tell her the rest," he says to Austin.

Bree frowns. "There's more?"

Austin clears his throat and looks at me. "These photos were taken two months ago," he says. "Charles Crawford has nothing to do with what's been happening to you."

"Oh."

Oh.

The cops exchange a look. Officer Leopold stands up and starts scooping the photos back into the envelope. "We really thought there was a good chance he could be behind this," he says. "A lot of the pieces fit, and the fact that he was unaccounted for seemed noteworthy."

"Right." I watch the last photo vanish into the envelope as Austin stands, too, then helps Bree to her feet.

"We've got officers driving past your house several times a day," he says. "In the meantime, we think it's safest for you to stay here. For you to keep a low profile while we try to figure out who the hell might want to mess with you."

Mark flinches at the word "hell," which seems strange. He gets to his feet and helps me up, steadying me in case my knees buckle.

"I'm okay," I assure him, assure them all. Bree's looking at me with concern in her eyes. "I'm fine."

Bree touches my arm. "It has to be a shock."

I nod, not sure what else to say. "It is." I look back at the cops. "Thank you for showing me the photos."

It sounds dumb when I say it out loud. Who in their right mind would be grateful for images of a dead ex-lover? But Austin just nods.

"It was self-defense," he says. "Apparently Crawford had been abusing his wife."

"So she shot him in the crotch." I can't say I'm sorry, or that I'm even surprised. Mark's watching me like he's unsure how to respond.

"We'll let you know if we learn anything else," Austin says, already headed for the door. "In the meantime, stay alert. Contact us immediately if you notice anything unusual."

Bree loops her arm through his, following him to the door. "We'll have extra security watching this cabin," she says. "You can feel safe here, okay?"

"Okay."

The cops and Bree make their way to the door, and I let them out, babbling pleasantries I'm only half hearing. When Mark closes the door behind them, he leans back against it and looks at me.

"How are you really?"

"Fine." I step forward, tentatively at first. "I really am. But could I get a hug?"

I don't have to ask twice. He envelops me in those big, strong arms and strokes my hair without saying a word. It's the best thing in the world, and I think about how many guys would try to fill the silence with platitudes. They'd tell me things happen for a reason or issue some chest-thumping assurances about keeping me safe.

But not Mark Bracelyn. He just strokes my back like he's gentling a horse and holds me until I don't need to be held anymore.

I draw back at last and grab hold of his hands. I want to look him in the eye, but I'm not ready to break contact. "I'm not sad," I tell him. "Part of me is glad that someone who hurt me can't hurt anyone anymore."

"Understandable."

"But I do feel—untethered. Like something's shifted in my universe, and I'm not sure what to do about it."

His brown eyes hold mine, compassion tethering us together. "You thought it was him," he says softly. "You thought Crawford was behind everything."

"Yeah," I admit. "I guess I did. I mean, it sorta made sense."

Not all the pieces fit, but still. Who else could possibly want to terrorize me?

A shiver ripples up my arms, and I hope Mark doesn't notice.

"The police will figure it out," he says. "And in the meantime, I've got you. We all do."

"Thanks."

We stand there like that for a long time. A clock ticks on the wall, but we don't let go of each other's hands. We stare into each other's eyes with heat growing between us. I know I'm not the only one feeling it. I can see it in his eyes like a kettle of dark chocolate going from a slow simmer to a hard boil.

"Mark." My voice is so husky I almost don't recognize it. "Will you—"

"Yes."

A smile tugs the edges of my mouth. "How do you know what I was going to ask?"

"I just do."

And he does. It's in his eyes, he wants me as much as I want him.

"Then do it." I lick my lips, hoping to God we're on the same page. That he's not thinking it's time to unload the dishwasher while I'm wanting him to— "Make love to me," I breathe. "Right now. Take me to your room and throw me back on the bed and make me forget there are men in the world who'd use their strength for bad instead of good."

I haven't even gotten all the words out when Mark scoops me into his arms. He picks me up like I weigh nothing at all, crushing his mouth against mine as he carries me to a side of the house I haven't seen yet. As he shoulders the door open on the master suite, I'm grateful this room is far away from where Libby sleeps.

He tosses me back on the bed and prowls over me. "What you said the other night," he says, voice low and heated. "About liking it rough. When you were with your girlfriends you said—"

"Yes," I tell him. "That's what I want."

"Because I can be gentle," he says. "So fucking gentle you wouldn't believe I'm the same guy."

I shake my head and reach down to tug my shirt over my head. "I don't want gentle," I tell him. "I want you."

His eyes flash, and I know he understands. Right now, I need to be possessed. I want to be claimed and overpowered and convinced there's someone big and powerful in control of everything, at least for a little while.

He kisses me again, hard this time, his tongue grazing mine as he pushes me back onto the bed. His hand covers my breast, squeezing and stroking until I arch up and moan against his mouth.

The instant my back leaves the mattress, he reaches under me to unhook my bra. He flicks it open with one hand, baring me to him. Lowering his mouth, he licks and sucks and devours me until I'm breathless and panting.

"Take it off," I growl as I claw at his shirt. "I need to see you."

He's reluctant to let go of my breasts, but he does it. I've never seen a guy unbutton a shirt so fast, and then it's flying across the room with his T-shirt.

Angling up on my elbows, I trace my fingers over the scar. He doesn't flinch, doesn't say a word, but he doesn't move away, either. A silent understanding shimmers between us with no words at all.

I see you. Scars and all, I see you and I want you.

Then he's kissing me again, kissing me as he unfastens my jeans and I claw at his and we somehow manage to get each other's pants off with our lips still fused together. My hands find their way into the front of his boxers, and I gasp against his mouth.

He draws back, hesitant for the first time since this started. "We can go slow," he says. "Or not at all if you're worried about—"

"No." I lick my lips and tighten my fist around him, making his eyes close. "A huge cock is not a problem."

His pupils dilate, and he gives a quick nod. Message received. I'm not kidding about wanting things a little dirty, a little rough.

Mark stands up and goes over to the bedroom door. He pushes it shut and flips the lock, then walks over to the nightstand. "You can tell me no at any time," he says. "Even after we're—once I'm—"

"I know," I tell him. And I do. There aren't many things I know with absolute certainty, but the fact that Mark would never hurt me is one of them.

My hips are already lifting as he sheathes himself with the condom. I'm squirming and panting and yes, stealing a quick glance at the condom wrapper for the expiration date.

Yeah, I've been burned before.

"Just bought 'em yesterday," Mark says, reading my mind. Which is scary as hell, or maybe it isn't. There's something wonderful about not needing to talk through every detail, to share every thought out loud if I want to be understood. Mark just gets me.

My legs fall open, and he moves between them, his hips wide and solid. I've never been with a man this big before, and the weight of him on my chest is deliciously overpowering. Bracing himself on his forearms, he stares into my eyes. His pupils swim in a molten sea of chocolate as he searches my eyes and grazes my slick core.

"Chelsea." He closes his eyes, and I realize that's the entirety of his statement. Just my name, whispered like a prayer as he slides into me.

"Oh, God." I cry out as he fills me to bursting. He's moving slowly, but the shock of it steals my breath away while my thighs clench instinctively to pull him deeper. I arch up, eager to meet his slow, powerful thrusts.

His eyes open again, and we're locked in each other's gazes, moving together like this is a choreographed dance we've practiced for years. I clutch at his shoulders, grateful we're face to face. I've never been one for eye contact during sex, for the weighty intimacy that comes with it. But it's different with Mark, and I have no idea how he makes me feel both cherished and conquered at the same time.

"Chelsea." There's an urgency in the word this time. "You feel so good."

"So do you." My words slur as he hits something really good, and I practically levitate off the bed. *"Yes."*

He smiles and keeps moving, slow and steady and so deep it takes my breath away. I angle up to kiss his scar, skimming my lips over its smooth ridges. His breath goes ragged, and I don't know if it's the kisses or the delicious friction between us that's causing it. All I know is that I'm close. The sensation's building like a roar in my ears, like the thunder of a charging army.

"Mark!" I bite down on his shoulder as the first wave hits. My body bows up to meet him, and I cry out again. "Oh, God."

He's right there with me; I can tell by the way he drives in harder and growls my name. I'm humming with pleasure, panting and clenching and clinging to him like he's my lifeboat in a churning ocean. I swear to God I almost pass out.

Slowly, the sensation ebbs. He eases off me, trailing a hand down the length of my body as I lie there with my eyes closed and my whole system buzzing with glorious sensory overload.

"You have a great smile."

I open my eyes to see him peering down at me in wonder. I didn't even know I was smiling, but the way he's staring at me makes me grin wider.

"You're pretty damn good at making me smile," I tell him.

His laughter is a soft rumble as he rolls away to get rid of the condom. He's back in an instant, pulling the covers around us and cradling me against his chest. His big body curls around me like a protective shell.

My own shell is melting; I can feel it. Those walls I put up, the reservations I have, they're dissolving like a sugar cube in warm tea. I know that's corny, but I feel it happening, and I'm powerless to resist.

I slide slowly into dreamland, wondering if he feels the same.

CHAPTER 14

MARK

I wake to the smell of brewing coffee and the weird sense that something's shifted in my world. When I open my eyes, Chelsea's tiptoeing into the bedroom holding two mugs and wearing my favorite plaid shirt with the sleeves rolled up. The top three buttons are undone, revealing the fragrant hollow where I buried my face hours ago. Her face lights up when she sees me, and I wonder what the hell I did in a past life to deserve something this fucking fantastic.

"Morning," she whispers. "I hope it's okay I fed the rabbit."

"Thank you," I say, accepting one of the mugs from her as she climbs back into bed and snuggles up next to me. "Is Libby still asleep?"

"Out cold," she confirms. "Between the sleepover and the pool day and poker night with your friends, I'm betting she'll stay zonked for another couple hours."

I sip my coffee, grateful for the bitter warmth and the pressure of Chelsea's bare thigh against mine. I got up in the night and threw on a pair of boxers, figuring I'd rather not sprint naked from bed in the event of a fire or sick kid or crazy nutjob harassing my girlfriend.

Girlfriend.

The word slips through my subconscious before I realize I've been rolling it around like a marble in my palm. Is that how Chelsea would see us? I'm guessing most single moms don't leap into bed with guys they're not at least a little serious about, but what the hell do I know?

My mom had sleepovers. Not a lot, but some. It drove my dad crazy, but it's not like he had any claim to her. She was clear that she never planned to get married, at least not to him.

"What are you thinking?"

I glance at Chelsea and wonder what she read on my face. "Thinking about my mom."

"Really?" She tilts her head, and I wish I could go back and rewind and say something else. Admitting I'm thinking about my mother while sitting half-naked with a beautiful woman in the same bed where we had crazy, passionate sex all night might be a little creepy.

But I'm already waist deep in weird, so I keep wading. "You remind me of her a little."

If Chelsea's offended, she doesn't show it. Just watches my face like she's waiting for more. Her gaze skitters over my scar, and I wonder if I should tell her the story behind it.

But no, that would be douchey. I'm already at risk of seeming like some wannabe hero, so no sense making it worse. Besides, describing my mom's house fire doesn't paint her in the best light. It wasn't her fault she lit the candles on my birthday cake, thinking she heard me coming through the door. Not her fault she got to talking with the UPS guy, and the candles caught the curtains on fire and—hell, anyway, I know it sounds bad.

And I want Chelsea to like my mom.

How's that for crazy; I'm already thinking of introducing her to my mother?

Chelsea's still watching me, like she's waiting me out or something. I lift my mug and chug half the coffee in two gulps, intent on keeping my mouth shut so I don't say something dumb.

"You've said you really like your mom," she says finally. "So, I guess that's a good thing if I remind you of her?"

"Definitely," I say, glad she's not pissed. "I don't mean it in a creepy way. Just that you're both smart and funny and strong as hell."

She smiles, biting her lip the way she does when she's got something on her mind. There's a stiffness in her shoulders that wasn't there a second ago, and I wonder if I'm totally botching this morning after thing.

"Everything okay?" I ask.

She looks up from her coffee, and there's that smile again, like a spear of sunshine to my heart. "I feel amazing," she says. "Last night was—it was so—God, listen to me." She laughs. "It was so fantastic I can't even find words."

"I'm glad." Not that she's wordless, but that it was even half as amazing for her as it was for me. "I loved it, too."

She's still smiling as she takes a sip of coffee, but that stiffness is still there. It's like she's curling in on herself even though she's leaned against me.

"I don't regret it at all," she says, and my heart balls up into wad of wet tissue paper.

I hold my breath, waiting for the *but.* I know there's a *but;* I can see it in her eyes.

"But?" I prompt, needing to rip off the damn Band-Aid.

"No, it's not like that." She tucks her hair behind her ear. When she drops her hand, it comes to rest on my thigh. "I just—I have a history of getting too serious about someone before we've really opened up to each other. Spilled our guts or whatever. You know what I mean?"

My breath stalls in my chest. Has she guessed my secret? Did she notice last night how Sean and James and Jonathan and even Bree look so much alike, while I—

"I want to tell you something, okay?" Her words come out fast, like she's ripping off her own Band-Aid. "It's—kind of a big deal. And I'm afraid you're going to think less of me, so I just need to get it out there and—"

"Chelsea, no." I curl my fingers around hers. "It doesn't matter what it is. I promise I won't think less of you."

The look she gives me is hopeful, and I almost feel bad about the relief that's coursing through me. I'm off the hook for spilling my secrets if she's got one she needs to get off her chest.

"You can't really promise that," she says. "You don't know what I'm going to say."

"What, you're a member of a satanic cult?" I shrug. "I'm sure they're nice people."

She laughs and shakes her head. "Not quite."

"You're a serial killer?" I picture Chelsea with a ski mask and a machete and have to struggle to keep a straight face. "I'm sure you only kill people who deserve it."

Her smile is more relaxed now, and I'm grateful she's easing up. "What, like Dexter?"

"Sure." I take a sip of coffee. "I might draw the line if you admit to slaughtering bunnies for sport, but other than that, you can tell me anything."

Her smile wobbles a little as she takes a deep breath. "It's about Libby's father," she says. "Biological father."

And judging by her expression, this is not a feel-good story. I lace my fingers through hers, channeling as much strength as possible into the gesture. "Okay."

She looks down into her coffee and a fist of panic grabs hold of my chest. *She's still in love with him. They're secretly married. He's actually her brother.*

So many worst-case scenarios are racing through my brain that I almost miss the next thing she says.

"Walter Grassnab. *Senator* Grassnab." Her gaze lifts to mine, and the vulnerability there makes my chest ache. "That's Libby's dad."

"Motherfucker."

She starts to draw her hand back, stung by what must sound like judgement. "That's not how I meant it," I insist, tightening my hold on her. "Him. Bree made me read his bio so we're all up to speed for this event. He's been married for twenty-five years, so—"

"That makes me an adulteress." The sound that escapes her is more of a shuddery little sob than a laugh, and she shakes her head. "Or an idiot. Probably both."

"You're neither," I insist, wishing she'd stop beating herself up. "Tell me the rest."

She takes a deep breath, staring down into her coffee like the answers are somewhere at the bottom. Her eyes are glittery when she meets mine again. "We met at a charity thing," she says. "He wasn't a senator then. Just a county commissioner, and I was in charge of pastries for the event. He came over to say he liked my cupcakes, and we started talking. I didn't have a clue who he was."

"I couldn't name any county commissioners, either," I offer. "Don't feel bad."

But it's clear she's feeling bad, and there's not a damn thing I can do to stop that. All I can do is listen and support, so I shut my trap and squeeze her hand.

"He was actually very sweet." She says it like that's a bad thing. "Charming and funny and I was still pretty raw from the breakup with Charlie." She takes a shaky breath and looks down into her mug again. "I fell right into bed with him like an idiot. I had no idea he was married. When he told me afterward, he swore they were getting divorced. Like a dummy, I believed him."

The pain in her voice makes my chest ache. I wonder which she hates more—what happened, or what she thinks it says about her.

"It wasn't your fault, Chelsea." My voice makes her look up

again, and I infuse it with every ounce of certainty I can. "He took advantage."

"I was a grownup," she says. "And I should have known better. For crying out loud, it's the oldest cliché in the book. Older, married man beds naïve, younger woman; forgets to mention a wife; swears it's over with her; etcetera etcetera. God."

The pain in Chelsea's eyes almost undoes me. If I could drive to the Senator's house right now and punch him in the nose, I'd do it. What a fucking asshole.

"So, he's Libby's father," I say.

She winces. "Biologically speaking, yes. Really more of a sperm donor."

For a second, I consider telling her about my father. It's the opposite story in some ways, a guy who didn't actually sire me but took credit anyway. I imagine what that would feel like, putting it out there. I've never told anyone in my life, never wanted to.

I don't want to now.

Besides, this is her story. Her moment.

"I didn't name him on the birth certificate," she says, answering a question I didn't think to ask. "By the time I realized he had all these huge political ambitions, I wanted to keep Libby as far away from that as I could. The last thing I'd want for her is to be trotted out as some slimy politician's dirty little secret."

Rage boils in the center of my chest, and I'm not sure where it's coming from. The idea that someone—anyone—could see Libby that way has me itching to punch a hole in the wall. And the idea that this creep of a senator could treat Chelsea that way—

"Fucking asshole," I growl.

She shakes her head and looks down again. "He doesn't even know about her," she says softly. "He broke things off before he knew I was pregnant. Before *I* knew."

Holy shit.

"He doesn't deserve her," I growl. "A guy who'd screw around on his wife and kids—that's not someone you want in her life anyway."

"Right," she says, brushing the hair from her eyes. "She's better off not being raised by him."

Is that why my mother never married Cort Bracelyn? She knew that deep down, he could only ever be a subpar father. Oh, he tried, but his heart wasn't in it, even though mine was.

"Mark?" Chelsea's voice is wary. "What are you thinking?"

Now. This is when I should tell her. Open up to her the way other guys haven't.

But I chicken out.

If I say it out loud, it's real, and I'm not ready for it to be real.

"Wait," I say as another thought occurs to me. "You're sure Senator Assgrab doesn't know about Libby?"

"How would he?" she asks. "We never saw each other again. Never spoke, and we don't exactly run in the same circles."

That's when I see it. The flicker of doubt in her eyes. She's saying one thing, but there's a thread of uncertainty wiggling through her words.

This is what she's been holding back.

"I think we should tell Austin," I say slowly. "And so do you."

My words hang there between us, suspended in the itchy tension.

Slowly, she nods. "Maybe." She releases a slow breath that's more resignation than relief. "It seemed like everything pointed to Charlie. Like maybe there was no need to say anything."

"You think it's possible." It's a statement, not a question, but I give her a chance to correct me. "That he found out about Libby or—?"

I trail off there because it seems like a dick move to say, "the father of your child has been fucking up your life." The words are implied, aren't they?

She considers it for a moment, then shakes her head. "I don't think so," she says. "I don't think he knows, and I don't think—" she laughs, but it's a hollow, bitter laugh. "After we split, he blocked me from all his social media. I heard he even changed his phone number. I'm not kidding when I say we've had zero contact."

I consider the kinds of crap Chelsea's tormentor has been pulling. Vandalism. Breaking and entering. "Just a guess, but Senator Assgrab doesn't seem like the type of guy to get his hands dirty."

"He's not," she says. "Not at all. Besides, what would he have to gain?"

Good point. She's kept her mouth shut for seven years, so why would he start dicking her around now? I study her face. Her words have me convinced, but there's a furrow between her brows that tells me she's hearing the same voice I am. That niggling little "what if" in the back of her brain.

"Austin needs to know," I say again. "All of it. He needs all the facts to investigate."

Her jaw clenches, and for a second, I think she's going to argue. That I'll have to choose between keeping my trap shut and keeping her safe. That's assuming Senator Assgrab really has anything to do with this, and who the hell knows if that's true?

She's quiet for so long I think I've lost her. "I've spent seven years keeping this secret," she says so softly I almost don't catch all the words. "There's always been gossip in town about who Lib's father is. For a while, there was even a rumor she was Austin's."

I wonder if Bree ever heard that. Or Austin.

"Putting 'father unknown' on that birth certificate made me feel like a horrible person," she admits. "Like who the hell doesn't know the father of her own child?"

There. This is my opening. My chance to come clean to Chelsea, to tell her my biggest secret. To open up the way I know I ought to if we're going to get anywhere together.

But I answer like a big, fat, fucking chicken. "You're not a horrible person," I tell her. "You're the kindest, smartest, most generous person I've ever met, and you did what you had to do to protect your daughter."

Tears flood her eyes, but she doesn't let any of them spill. She leans into me, her hair tickling my bare chest. I slip my arm around her, pulling her close enough so I can breathe in the scent of her skin. My whole life, I've never felt this close to another person.

There's plenty of time to tell her my own secrets, to open up the way she's been asking.

"It's going to be okay," I murmur as I stroke her hair. "Let's call Austin."

* * *

BY THE TIME Chelsea's done spilling her guts at the police station, I don't know who I admire more: Her for unflinchingly telling her cop ex about the married man she slept with, or Austin for not being a dick about it.

I'm guessing plenty of cops would get pissy with her for not coming forward sooner, but Austin just sits with his hands folded on his desk and nods like he's been expecting her to drop by.

"Thank you for telling me this," Austin says. "I promise you I'll do as much as I can to safeguard your secret."

"Libby's secret," I add, in case he didn't get the full point of why she did this.

"Libby's secret," Austin says, looking at me for a few beats longer than comfortable. "You're right, a child's paternity is something intensely personal to families, but no one more than that child."

Pretty sure I'm imagining the way he looked right at me when he said that. I hope I am, anyway. Bree's complained about Austin's mind-reading abilities, and right now, I don't doubt it.

But he turns his attention back to Chelsea and addresses her in what Bree calls his Officer Velvet Voice tone. "When was the last time you had contact with Senator Grassnab?" he asks.

"Seven years ago on January eighteenth," she says. "I remember because he came by to tell me we couldn't see each other anymore. That he was working things out with his wife. And it was exactly one week later that I realized my period was late, so I went and bought a test."

He doesn't flinch at her candor, which makes me like him more. And her, for putting it all out there like this. She's sitting up straight in her chair, and the only sign she's uncomfortable is the tenseness of her fingers wrapped in mine.

I give her hand a squeeze and clear my throat. "Is the men's room down the hall?"

I know damn well where the men's room is, and I'm guessing Austin knows I know. "Yeah," he says, not missing a beat. "Fourth door on the left."

"Thanks." I squeeze Chelsea's hand again, then let go. "I'll be right back."

I feel their eyes on me as I go, but no one says anything. As the door swings shut behind me, the murmur of voices starts up again. I can't make out the words, and I don't try to. Just a hunch, but I'm guessing there's some personal shit Austin needs to ask her. Things she might be uncomfortable sharing in front of a guy she's just started dating. If it means better odds of solving this crime, I'll give them all the privacy they need.

Slipping my phone out of my pocket, I notice I missed a call from Bree. A flutter of worry wiggles behind my breastbone, and I push my way through the exit at the end of the corridor. We left Bree in charge of Libby, and even though I know my sister's good with kids, my chest knots with worry as I dial her number.

She answers on the first ring. "Is your rabbit supposed to eat cereal?"

"Uh, hello to you, too."

Libby's voice rings out in the background, singing Alice the Camel at full volume. The knot releases in my chest as my sister keeps talking.

"I'm calling because Libby found your stash of disgusting sugar cereal and asked to have some," she says. "I was going through the boxes trying to figure out what's least unhealthy and she pulled out the Trix and said she needed to feed Long Long Peter. Are you seriously feeding this crap to your rabbit?"

"Silly rabbit," I say at the same time I hear Libby chant the exact same words in the background. "Trix are for kids."

Bree goes silent. "Okay, that was freaky."

"Have you seriously never heard that television commercial?" I know my sibs went to elite boarding schools and spent weekends doing English riding lessons and tennis instead of parked in front of the television watching cartoons, but sometimes it's like we grew up on different planets.

"So I'll take that as an ixnay on pouring a bowl of cereal for the rabbit," Bree says. "That was my guess, but I figured I'd better check it with the authorities."

The fact that she's deemed me an authority on children freaks me out a little, but I don't let on. "Rabbit chow is in the cupboard beside the sink."

"Got it," she says. "Are things going okay?"

It's killing her not to pry. For someone who loves meddling in other people's lives as much as Bree does, it's gotta be rough living with a cop. But she rushed right over when we called this morning and asked her to stay with Libby. She only asked the bare minimum of questions, even though it had to drive her nuts.

"You're coming to the meeting tomorrow night, right?" she asks.

"For fuck's sake."

"That's a yes?"

I scrub my hand over my beard. "Why do we have so many damn meetings?"

"We're the owners of a multi-million-dollar resort that's just getting off the ground," she points out. "Call me crazy, but I think we should get together and talk about it occasionally."

I consider pointing out that it's my birthday and that the last thing I want is to be stuck in a damn boardroom. But birthdays aren't a big deal to me. A shrink would probably spout some bull-shit story about the trauma associated with childhood birthday parties, or maybe with the whole "candles lit the house on fire" thing, but I'd rather not dwell on that. Frankly, my idea of a perfect birthday is pizza and cake with Chelsea and Libby and not a single damn candle to blow out.

"Fine," I mutter, crossing my fingers it's a fast meeting and I can still pull off the pizza and cake thing. "Thanks again for watching Libby."

"Thanks for giving me a chance to play auntie," she says. "For the record, I'm totally on board if you want to make it an official thing."

"What, like being her nanny?"

"You're such an idiot sometimes." At least she says it with affection. "You'd make a good stepdad, you know. Husband, too, for that matter."

Jesus. "Because I had such great role models for that?"

"Some people get the benefit of learning from positive examples," she says. "But most of us get to learn from screwups—ours or someone else's. Doesn't matter much how you get there, as long as you learn."

"Is this psychology session almost over?"

Being a jackass doesn't make the lump in my throat go away, but Bree's laughter does. "I love you, dumbass."

She hangs up before I can reply.

CHAPTER 15

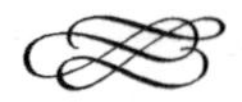

CHELSEA

I'm betting Austin knows as well as I do that Mark's bathroom run was just a cover for giving us some privacy. It was a sweet gesture, though there's really not much I wouldn't say in front of Mark. Not now, anyway, and I feel a tingly tug in my chest at the thought of being this close to another person. This hasn't happened in—well, forever.

Austin leans back in his chair, his posture all cool-cop casual. "Is there anything else you want to share?" he asks. "Anything you think might help the case?"

I shake my head slowly, tumbling the thoughts around in my brain. "No," I say. "For what it's worth, I don't think he's behind this."

"Senator Grassnab?"

"Right." I scrape my thumbnail over a speck of something that looks like vanilla fondant on the edge of Austin's desk. "I just don't picture him doing something like this."

Austin's eyes hold mine for a long time. "I'm guessing you also didn't picture him having a wife." His voice is kind, but the words sting anyway. "Just like I'm guessing you never imagined Charlie Crawford had a history of abuse."

"Ouch."

"Sorry." The sympathy in his eyes stings even more. "If there's one thing I've learned in this job, it's that people are capable of a lot of things you'd never expect."

"No, you're right." I force myself not to glance toward the door, toward the hallway where Mark disappeared. "I guess I have some history of picking guys who aren't super-forthcoming."

Austin lifts an eyebrow. "You have concerns?"

Well, I didn't until you started reminding me of all my past fuckups...

But no, that's not what Austin's doing. He's a good guy who's just doing his job, and I'm the one reading too much into things.

"Mark's amazing," I tell him, wanting to put that out there up front. "Brave and strong and kind and tender and—"

"I might need to stop you there," he says, grimacing. "There are some things a guy doesn't need to know about his poker buddies."

"Right," I say, getting on with it. "It's just—sometimes I feel like he's hiding stuff from me."

Austin folds his hands on the desk and studies me. "Just to play devil's advocate, I suppose he could have said the same until this morning when you told him about Libby's father."

Fair point. "I guess that's what I mean, though. I spilled my deepest, darkest secrets, and he told me jack about himself. I don't even know if he's ever had a serious girlfriend."

"Have you tried asking him?"

Again, he has a point. I hate that. "You're right," I say. "I guess I can't expect someone to give me something I've never actually asked for."

"Don't feel bad; I've had to learn that one the hard way myself."

Ah, Bree. I forget sometimes that things haven't always been perfect roses and sunshine for them.

"And I guess we've only barely started dating," I say. "Maybe he'll open up."

Austin nods. "Sure, it's possible."

Is it? I'm not convinced, but I nod anyway. "Thanks, Austin. You've given me some good things to think about."

"Let me give you one more." He steeples his hands together, his expression impassive. "Dating a Bracelyn is like riding on the luggage carousel at the airport. It's exciting and fun and makes you feel like you're getting away with something insanely cool. But there's a helluva lot of baggage there."

"That might be the weirdest metaphor I've ever heard in my life."

He smiles. "Bracelyns don't open up easily," he says. "When they do, you know it's because they see a future with you. Be patient."

"Good advice." I pick at the spot on his desk, pretty sure it's paint and not fondant. I miss my bakery. "Ever thought you should have been a shrink?"

He grins. "Nope."

"Or a couples' therapist?"

"Definitely not." His smile reminds me why I dated him way back when, and why I'm thrilled to bits he and Bree found each other.

"I guess your talents are best used catching bad guys, huh?" The door opens, and my heart does a delighted shimmy as Mark strides through.

Austin nods and folds his hands on the desk. "Let's hope it happens soon."

* * *

BEFORE WE'VE LEFT the parking lot, Mark gets stuck on an emergency call with his brother—something about a malfunction in the golf course sprinklers—so I end up driving us back to the resort while he barks words like "discharge tube" and "ball check valve" and I try not to snicker like a twelve-year-old boy.

Libby pounces the instant we get back to the resort, giddy with the promise of more pool time and a horseback ride at the resort's stables.

All that to say there's little time in my day for a private, adult conversation with Mark. Austin's right, I need to ask questions. I can't expect Mark to open the door if I've never knocked.

I'm zonked by the time Libby's tucked into the guest room of Mark's cozy little cabin. Zonked but happy. It's so peaceful here. Crickets and coyote song hum in the distance, but other than that, it's quiet. Mark's bedroom smells like the cinnamon potpourri Bree sneaks into every nook and cranny when she visits, determined to make her brother's space homier.

I sit down on the edge of Mark's bed and breathe it all in, grateful for the unexpected calm in the center of my chest. Grateful for everything Mark's done for us over the last couple weeks.

The man himself ambles into the bedroom holding two glasses of wine and a bottle labeled "lemon-sage massage lotion." His bare chest and low-slung boxers are all it takes to jettison the exhaustion from my brain, not to mention any thoughts of grownup conversation. The sight of all that muscle and flesh has me craving another sort of grownup activity.

"Massage?" He hands me one of the glasses and sets the other on his nightstand.

"Giving or receiving?" I ask. "Either way, the answer's yes."

He eases onto the bed beside me. "Giving," he says. "Bree told me you were crazy about this massage lotion the other night, so I grabbed some at the spa."

Two massages in twenty-four hours? I don't know how I got this lucky, but I can't stop looking at his hands. "Something tells me you're good at this," I tell him. "Strong hands, impressive stamina—all the tools of a great amateur masseur."

He shrugs and flips the top open on the bottle. "I've never had complaints."

And there's my opportunity. My chance to nudge him into opening up about his personal life, his dating history.

I tug my T-shirt over my head and unhook my bra, basking in the hunger that flickers through his eyes. Shucking my shirt will make the massage easier, sure, but it's also a good way to make sure Mark's feeling nice and cheerful.

I'm not proud.

"So," I begin as I pull my hair to one side and ease onto my stomach. "I imagine you've massaged a girlfriend or two?"

That came out more awkward than I meant it to.

But it was still subtle, right? The door is open for him to share, to tell me more about his past. I can't see his face with my forehead pressed into the pillow, but I feel him moving behind me, considering the question, preparing to share.

Sppppplurt.

The flatulent outburst has me craning my neck to see. Behind me, Mark gives a sheepish look. "Lotion bottle was clogged."

"Oh."

Okay, so much for subtlety. I press my forehead back into the pillow, reconsidering my tactic. Maybe a more direct approach.

My thoughts go sideways as his hands connect with my back. His palms feel even more massive than normal as they knead and stroke and work the lotion into my knotted muscles. I release a breath I didn't know I was holding, breathing in the calming scent of sage and citrus. God, that feels good.

"Tell me about your first girlfriend, Mark." I force out the words before I forget them completely. "Or your most serious relationship."

He doesn't say anything right away, but that's normal for Mark. I wait, stifling a groan as he strokes the heels of his hands into the knots between my shoulder blades. "You want me to talk about other women while you're naked and I'm touching you?"

"I'm still wearing shorts. Not naked." Which is totally not the point. My brain is too bliss-fogged right now to think straight.

"Better fix that," he says, and tugs the flimsy cotton sleep shorts down my thighs.

Oh, God. His forearm just grazed my ass and I drooled on the damn pillow. This is not how I saw this going.

"There." He tosses the shorts aside and skates both palms slowly from my bared thighs over my ass, his caress gentler than I ever imagined a big man could be. "Easier to get your low back now."

I try again to stifle a groan but fail this time. Whatever he's doing to my low back is uncoiling knots I never knew were there. The pleasure is otherworldly.

"I want to know more about you," I murmur into the pillow, determined to have this conversation. "That was a pretty big secret I spilled this morning. Maybe you can share one of yours?"

More silence, which might be annoying if his fingertips weren't deftly squeezing every last needle of stress from the center of my back. I let out a breath, which escapes as more of a moan. Yesterday's massage was great, but being touched this way by a man who knows my body inside and out—

"Cari Ann Eliott," he says.

I blink open my eyes. "What?"

"Girlfriend," he says. "You asked."

Oh. "Right, of course."

I wait to see if there's more, but that seems to be it. He goes back to stroking and kneading and *ohmygod right there*—

"Yep." The single, grunted syllable floods me with hope. There's more coming, a new openness in our relationship.

"Third grade," he continues, and I try not to feel disappointed. "I gave her the applesauce from my lunch. It was true love until she fell off the monkey bars at recess and broke her arm and then her family moved to Pittsburgh."

That was quite possibly the longest string of words I've ever heard from Mark. It's progress, but not quite what I'd hoped for.

Have you tried asking him?

Austin's words echo in my head, and I realize I need to be more specific. More direct with my questions. "Tell me about your scar," I say. "The one on your chest. How did you get it?"

He's quiet again, focused on the tangle of knots where my bra straps normally rest. Oh, dear Lord, that feels wonderful. He's using his thumbs to erase the tension, rubbing and coaxing the knotted muscle until it slowly gives up and relaxes.

"Fire," he says, pulling me out of my bliss coma. "When I was a teenager."

"Oh." What was the question again?

The scar, right, his scar.

I already knew about the fire, thanks to Bree, but I'm still hoping for more. "What happened?" I ask.

"Flaming two-by-four right to the chest," he says.

Good God. "I'm so sorry."

"Mpf," he says, and I hold my breath waiting for the rest of the story. "How's this pressure?"

"What?"

He strokes the heels of his hands along the edges of my spine, releasing the tension there. Another groan escapes me.

"The pressure," he says again. "Too hard?"

"God, no."

My response comes out a lot breathier than I mean it to, but I can't help it. His fingertips just grazed the edges of my breasts and now I'm tingling in spots that are nowhere near where he's rubbing.

He makes a sound that's almost a chuckle and keeps rubbing. "Your skin is so soft," he murmurs. "Right here especially."

I shiver as he grazes the sides of my breasts again, stoking every nerve ending from an ember to a low-burning flame. I don't know if it's a muscle or a tendon or some other anatomical feature along my rib cage, but whatever he's doing to it is pure magic.

Where were we again?

Childhood memories. Right. Or something like that.

"Favorite childhood Halloween costume."

That was dumb. It was the first thing that popped into my head, but maybe it'll work. Maybe I'll gain some unexpected insight into his personality. Some sweet, cherished memory that tells me who he is.

"Pirate," he says. "I was seven. My mom made the whole costume by hand."

Mmm, now we're getting somewhere. His answers, not what he's doing with his fingertips in those sensitive little hollows between my ribs, though that's amazing, too.

I command myself to stay focused on the conversation, to pull myself out of the sage-scented clouds and concentrate on his memories. I picture seven-year-old Mark with an eyepatch and a plastic hook hand, but my brain gets muddled by the feel of his real hands stroking closer to my breasts again. I don't mean to, but I catch myself arching up to grant more access to my breasts.

Wait, this wasn't the plan.

But I don't fight it as his fingers glide closer to my nipples, and *ohmygod,* this man should have his hands bronzed. But then he couldn't do what he's doing now, which is the most amazing thing I've ever felt. I gasp out loud as my core turns to molten liquid.

Did I mention he's really fucking good at this?

"Libby asked for a pirate-themed birthday party," I blurt.

I'm totally botching this, but I can't seem to stop blurting stupid things. I want to keep the conversation flowing, but these are not the heartfelt, probing discussion points I'd practiced. What were those again?

My brain's still snagged on pirates, and I imagine Mark as a pirate. *Rugged, rough, possessive with strong hands and—*

"Her birthday is in June," I continue like an idiot. "But she's already picked out all the party favors. And the cupcakes. Pink melon with perky little gumdrop nipples."

"What?"

Ugh. I just made my daughter's birthday cupcakes sound porny. I'm a terrible mother.

"Gumdrops," I manage, not sure why the hell I'm talking about this. "I bake gumdrops inside the cupcakes, and they're like little jewels for the kids to find."

"Sounds nice."

"It will be."

Oh, God, kill me now. I should just shut up. I won't be able to form words much longer anyway, since he's moved to that tense spot behind my ears. His thumbs circle in slow, deliberate swirls, teasing the tight bundle of nerves into submission.

This is hands down the best massage of my life.

"You should come," I groan.

Mark's hands go still. "What?"

I've already forgotten what I said, and it takes a few beats to scroll back through my own words. *Oh.*

"To the party," I clarify, though part of me wants to just go with the other meaning. "You should come to the party."

"Mmm." I can't tell if that's a noncommittal response or a groan of pleasure. Wait, I *can* tell. He's leaning forward to press deeper into my shoulder muscles and there's a hard bulge pressing into my tailbone.

Either that's the lotion bottle in his boxers, or he's as turned on as I am.

My subconscious fights to resurface. I know I should be frustrated. For God's sake, we're talking about birthday parties, and he hasn't once mentioned his thirtieth is tomorrow? It's a bad sign, I know it is, but at the moment, I can't wrap my brain around why. The hard, hot length of him is pressed against my back, his warm breath coaxing the nerves behind my earlobe into a full-fledged sizzle.

Oh, God.

I moan again, fighting my body's response, fighting to follow through on the conversation I know we need to have.

Why was that again?

"Give it," I groan, my subconscious still focused on secrets while the rest of me demands something else. My thighs move apart, and Mark slips into the space between them. His teeth graze the nape of my neck, and I groan again with the delicious weight of him, the splendor of being pinned beneath all that glorious heat.

"Chelsea?" he breathes against my earlobe.

"Mmm?"

"If you want, we can keep talking about house fires and candy and childhood crushes," he says. "Or if you want—"

"I want," I groan as my traitorous backside arches up to grind against him. "I want you so much."

My own body is betraying me, I know it. But as Mark kneads my breasts with one hand while the other tears open the crinkly condom wrapper, I can't bring myself to fight it.

As he slides into me from behind, I forget it all. My questions, my fears, my doubts, my worries that this whole thing is going to explode in a flaming ball of hurt and betrayal.

CHAPTER 16

MARK

I'm an asshole, okay?

I know Chelsea was fishing for personal stuff last night, and I'm a grade-A dick for not sharing.

At best she thinks I'm clueless, incapable of reading signals or carrying on normal human conversation.

At worst she thinks I'm a closed-off prick who can't open up to her.

Either way, it's better than the truth.

I'll choose those things over having her know that deep down, I'm just a chickenshit, emotionally-clobbered kid who's fucking terrified of losing his family and identity and place in the world. As much as I want her to know the whole me, to unburden myself to her the same way she's done with me, I'm not ready to have it be real. Not even in the privacy of my bedroom with the woman I love.

Yeah, I said it.

Not to her, because as I already mentioned, I'm an asshole.

But I'm in love with Chelsea, and I can't stop thinking about it as I stomp my way from my cabin across the resort grounds to the conference room where we're having yet another goddamn meeting about the golf course. Or about expanding the equestrian center or getting new soap at the day spa, I forget. I've had a lot on my mind lately, so much I forgot my own damn birthday and—

I stumble to a halt, tripping over my own feet outside the conference room. Holy shit. That's it, isn't it? That's why everyone's been acting weird. Bree, Sean, James, Jonathan—no fucking wonder they've been tiptoeing around, whispering like elves on Christmas morning.

My goddamn birthday.

For weeks I've been paranoid, but as I stand here with my hand on the doorknob, I know. I know what's about to happen, and I can't stop the stupid, pathetic, childish grin from spreading over my face. As I shove the door open, I've got my heart in my throat and a big, stupid ache in my—

"Surprise!"

I jerk back, even though I was braced for it. But I wasn't braced for all these people. Dozens of them, friends, family, neighbors. There's Jade and Amber from next door, and Bree singing happy birthday at the top of her lungs with all her girlfriends gathered around like backup dancers. My brothers are scattered through the crowd, Sean next to Amber, James leaned against a wall apart from the crowd, holding a glass of wine like he's at a dinner party. Jonathan's on the other side of the room shooting lustful glances at one of Bree's friends I haven't met yet.

I love everyone here, every single one of them, even the ones whose names I can't remember. I love that I'm a part of something bigger, that I've found my place in the world after a fucking lifetime of looking. My heart swells like a fist that's been smashed knuckles-first through a wall, and I stare at the crowd feeling like the luckiest bastard on earth.

"Holy shit." The words tumble out of me before I spot Libby at the edge of the room, Chelsea's hands on her shoulders. She's belting out happy birthday at the top of her lungs, complete with dance moves that put her Alice the Camel routine to shame.

If I thought my heart couldn't get any bigger, it just broke the fucking magnifying glass like that scene from the Grinch cartoon.

And there. Right next to Chelsea is my mother.

"Happy birthday, baby," she says as the song winds down. She steps forward to throw her arms around my middle, squeezing so tight I hiccup. "I'm so glad I can quit hiding. Your brothers and sisters have been sneaking me around this place all day."

"Mom," I murmur, hugging back as I breathe in the familiar smell of vanilla breath mints and lemon hand cream. The swelling in my chest is so fierce, so tender, that I can't catch my breath.

She pulls back and beams at me like she did when I won the fifth-grade spelling bee. "I can't wait to catch up." She casts a knowing smile at Chelsea and lowers her voice just a little. "I want to hear all about what's happening in your life. *Everything*."

Something tells me Bree's already taken care of that, but I don't mind. I'm glad to have this out in the open. To know all my favorite females in the world have been hanging out together and enjoying each other's company.

"Mom." My voice sounds weird and gravelly, so I clear my throat. "You've met Chelsea." I stop myself before I can add something dumb like "my girlfriend." We haven't talked about labels yet, so I know not to go slapping them on in front of my mother. "And Libby," I add as the girl extends her hand and tells my mom it's nice to meet her. "Libby's my friend, too."

Chelsea's smile wobbles, or maybe that's just Bree crashing into her from behind. "Oops, sorry." Bree pulls Chelsea in for one of those long, rocking hugs, then releases her and moves on to my mom. "Betty, I can't believe we pulled it off," she says. "The dummy had no clue."

"True enough," I admit, trying to catch Chelsea's eye. She's fussing with the bow on Libby's ponytail, so now's probably not the time to grab for her hand. "I'm impressed."

Bree grins and bumps my mom with her hip. "We've got mad skills," she says. "You must have thought we'd forgotten?"

I'd forgotten, but she already thinks I'm a dumbass, so I keep my mouth shut. "I'm so glad you're here," I say to all of them, but especially Chelsea. "Thank you."

She lifts her eyes then, and the warmth of her smile tells me I probably just imagined her funny expression a minute ago. "Happy birthday, Mark," she says. "I'll give you your present later."

Her voice is pitched with sweetness, so it's probably not something dirty, though I never know with Chelsea. That's what I love about her. The perfect mix of sweetness and sin, softness and sharp, sexy edge. I love all of it, every last drop.

Did I mention I love her?

The words are busting up out of my chest like an alien in the movies, which is probably the wrong damn image to have in mind when telling a woman I love her for the first time, so I keep my damn mouth shut.

My sister grabs my arm. "Before I forget, Senator Grassnab might be stopping by."

All the blood leaves my brain. From the corner of my eye, I see Chelsea stagger, but Bree keeps talking like she hasn't noticed a damn thing, and why would she? It's not like she knows Chelsea's secret.

"...big event isn't until tomorrow, but he came in a day early to enjoy some R and R before the big campaign launch," Bree's saying. "He's at dinner with Mrs. Grassnab now, but I invited him to stop by and say hello."

I fumble for my voice, hoping I can shape it into some appropriate words instead of the ones flying around in my head.

Fuck. Shit. Goddammit.

Get her out of here.

It takes everything in my power to keep my eyes off Chelsea, to not do anything that would alert my mom or Libby or Bree that a giant ball of what-the-fuck has just bowled through the room.

I need to get her out of here.

Reaching for Chelsea's hand, I twine my fingers through hers. I need her to know I've got her back.

She looks up at me with a smile that seems normal, but there's panic in her eyes. Her hand trembles in mine, but her expression is perfectly composed. If I didn't know her so well, I'd never guess anything's wrong.

"I'm going to take Libby over to the buffet for some food," she says, ruffling her daughter's hair. "We're a little off our schedule, so we probably can't stay too late."

Bless her little heart, Libby yawns. I know it's not an act, since the kid has to be exhausted as hell, but she couldn't have timed it better.

"You sleepy, kiddo?" I ask, struggling to keep my voice normal.

"No," she says, covering another yawn. "Maybe just a little. But I can stay up late."

"We'll see about that," Chelsea says with a smile at my mother that says *kids these days*. "I think it would do us all some good to get back on track with a normal bedtime routine."

"You won't hurt anyone's feelings if you slip out early," Bree assures her as she snags a glass of champagne from a passing waiter. "You and Mark have plenty of time later for gifts."

My mother's knowing smile says she knows damn well what my sister's implying. But my mom is nothing if not gracious, so she stoops down to Libby's level and smiles. "It's tough when you're the only kid at a party, huh? I run a preschool near Portland. Do you know where that is?"

Libby scrunches up her forehead and nods. "That's where the zoo is?"

"Exactly," my mother says. "I live right by there, and I just visited last week. They have a new baby owl hatchling there. Actually, I think he may have stowed away in my purse."

She reaches into the oversized bag slung across her body and pulls out a big-eyed, fuzzy plush bird. As she hands it over to Libby, the girl's eyes go owllike in wonder.

"That's for me?"

"It is," my mom confirms. "What do you think you should name him?"

Libby thinks about that. "Weird Owl Yankovic," she says. "He can be friends with Long Long Peter."

"That sounds like a wonderful idea to me," my mom says.

My heart is knotted up in a big heavy ball, but I know I need to stay focused on the impending crisis. Sweet as this whole exchange is, Chelsea's getting edgy. I can feel it in the way she grips my hand, in the way she keeps shooting glimpses at the door like she expects the senator to come barging through at any moment and point at her and Libby.

"Know what Libby hasn't seen yet?" I ask.

Clutching the owl to her chest, Libby swivels her gaze to me. "What?"

"The game room," I say. "It's got foosball and air hockey and video games and even a ball pit. There's lots of other kids your age, too. Want to see it sometime?"

"Yes. Yes yes yes *yes*!" Libby bounces with excitement, like this is the best damned day of her life. Maybe it is. She looks at her mother. "Can we go, Mom?"

"Let's grab some food and then we'll slip out." Chelsea shoots me a grateful look. "You're sure you don't mind?"

"Positive." My mom and Bree are distracted talking with Libby about the merits of air hockey versus foosball, so I lean close enough that my beard brushes Chelsea's ear. "You okay with leaving early?"

She nods with a big, stiff smile screwed on tight. "Bree let me help with setup, so I got to meet everyone. Your mom is great."

I try not to react, but she must see something in my face. "What?"

"Nothing," I assure her. "My mom *is* great."

"But?"

But she's not known for clamming up the way the Bracelyn clan is. No wonder she never wanted to marry into the family. I steal a glance at my mom, wondering what she's shared. If she's told Chelsea anything that could send her stumbling into my cesspool of secrets.

"But, nothing," I say, keeping my damned mouth shut.

She looks at me for a long time, like she's watching for something she's beginning to think might never actually happen. "You're sure?"

"Yep." I clear my throat. "Now go on, have fun with Libby. I'll see you back at the cabin?"

"Sure," she says, taking a step back.

It's the look on her face that twists the ball of my heart into a tighter knot. Hope, fear, and a bone-deep sadness I'm positive has nothing to do with the senator.

Putting her hand on Libby's back, she turns and walks away.

CHAPTER 17

CHELSEA

I clock a solid twenty minutes at the party, practically choking on my virgin mojito every time the door opens.

But I'm determined to make the rounds, to pretend everything's totally normal, and I'm carefree and cheerful about Mark's birthday instead of terrified my daughter's sperm donor will come busting through the door demanding explanations.

Austin eases my mind a little, catching my arm on my way out the door to murmur quiet assurances they've got an eye on Walter Grassnab. There's no evidence yet, but he's a person of interest, and that's enough to have cops prowling the resort tonight.

The game room is less than two hundred yards away, and I tow Libby across the lawn toward a cedar-sided structure marked Cottonwood Cabin. I'm breathless as we jog the paved path with the sun sinking behind us into a candy floss nest of clouds.

"Ow. Mom, you're squeezing my hand."

"Sorry, baby." I loosen my grip and smile down at her. "Did you have fun at the party?"

"It was good," she says. "I like Grandma Bootie."

"Who?"

"Mark's mom," she says. "She says all the kids at the preschool call her Grandma Bootie."

"Oh. That's—sweet."

I ignore the painful stabbing in the center of my heart. Libby and my mother aren't close. It's tough to forge a relationship with a woman who refers to you as "Chelsea's little accident." Not that Lib's ever heard that—I've made damn sure of it—but it goes without saying theirs isn't a tender connection.

But Mark's mom is different. Warm and sweet and welcoming, she pulled me into a big hug before Bree had even finished introducing us. "Bree's told me so much about you," Betty exclaimed as she released me and smiled so big I could see her molars. "We've been chatting for months about the party, so I got to hear all about how you two got together."

So, Bree, not Mark, told his mom about me. I shouldn't be surprised, or even disappointed. At least I'm not the only person he shuts out.

Libby's voice breaks through my noisy haze of uncertainty. "I love my owl," she says as she hugs it to her chest.

"He's a great owl." I push open the big wooden door and step into the foyer. The space is warm and bright, filled with children's laughter and the smell of popcorn.

Libby bounces beside me, revving her engine before she jets off toward the snack bar. She's still clutching my hand, so I stumble along in her wake. "Mom, can I have cotton candy? Or Skittles? I need—"

"You don't need any more sugar." I reel her in and redirect her toward a copper arrow marked "game room." We pass another mom being yanked along by sticky-faced twin toddlers, and we share a smile of solidarity.

"Where do you think we'll find the ball pit?" I ask Lib.

"This way!" Her gleeful enthusiasm lets some of the tension

leak from my shoulders. As much as I liked the party, it's good to escape the dread of running into Walter Grassnab.

We turn down a corridor and keep following the copper signs. Libby's buzzing with energy, courtesy of the massive slab of chocolate cake she gulped at the party. So much for an early bedtime.

"Maybe after the ball pit we get cotton candy?" she asks.

Gotta admire the kid's persistence. "No dice, kiddo. You already had cake."

"But there's still room in the sweets chamber of my tummy."

A delicate flutter under my breastbone reminds me these are Mark's words, Mark's influence on my little girl. Or maybe it's the reminder that he's let us into his world, at least a little.

We round the corner into a room humming with activity. Arcade games beep and buzz as kids scamper around us shouting with excitement. There's a fierce game of foosball happening on the other side of the room, and opposite that is the holy grail. The ball pit we've heard so much about. It's teeming with plastic balls in red and green and blue, a rainbow-hued pool of pure joy. A pre-schooler with a buzz cut squeals and leaps like he's jumping into a swimming pool.

"Whoa," Libby says.

"No kidding. Pretty nice, huh?"

"I wish we could live here forever."

"Here in this game room? Seems like it would be hard to sleep."

"Mom." She rolls her eyes, giving me a glimpse of the teenager she'll be before I know it. "With Mark. I think we should live with Mark forever."

There's that twinge again, twin darts of hope and trepidation pinning my heart like thumbtacks.

Don't get ahead of yourself. You've made that mistake before.

I'm giving myself this silent pep talk when a pigtailed girl maybe a year younger than Lib bounds over sporting purple cowboy boots and a huge smile that showcases a missing front tooth. "I'm Tia, what's your name?"

"I'm Libby," my daughter replies, fingers still clutching mine. "Do you live here?"

"No, we're on vacation," Tia says. "Do you want to play?"

"Okay." Libby looks up at me with hope-filled eyes. "Mom, can I?"

"Go for it. Have fun." Lord knows she's due for some peer interaction.

"Come on." Tia grabs my daughter's hand and off they go, skipping toward the ball pit. There's a teenager with a whistle around his neck standing guard at the edge of it, but I move closer anyway so I'm right there if she needs me.

"She's adorable."

I turn to see Mark's mother approaching, her friendly smile arched wide across her pretty features. "So smart for her age," she adds. "She counted to twenty for me in both English and Spanish."

"That sounds like Libby," I tell her. "Thank you for the owl, by the way."

"Don't mention it. I'm just tickled Mark's opened himself up to something new."

I'm not sure if she means me or Libby or relationships in general, but I nod like it's true. "He's a terrific guy. So supportive these last couple weeks."

Betty's face creases with concern. "Bree shared some of what's been happening to you. I'm so sorry."

There it is again. It's Bree who's told her about me, not Mark. Has he even said a word?

"Do you and Mark talk often?" I ask cautiously.

"Oh, every week. Such a good boy, always calling to ask what's happening in my life."

"And to share what's happening in his?"

She cocks her head, bemused. "Well, now. He did say he won ten dollars at poker night."

"That's—something."

"It's so nice he's made friends," she continues, turning her gaze back out over the ball pit where Libby's poised to leap. "Mark always did like being part of a family, part of a community."

I file that information away in the brain folder that contains surprisingly few facts about Mark. It's embarrassing how little I know about him.

"He's been terrific with Libby," I tell her. "Very protective."

"He gets that from Cort. Not much of a father figure, but hell-bent on supporting his kids the best way he knew how. Mostly with money, I guess."

Yet another tidbit of information to tuck into my file, along with what I've picked up from Bree. How is it possible I've learned none of this from Mark himself?

"I hope it's okay I told Libby to call me Grandma Bootie," she says, glancing back to me. "I didn't want to overstep, but it's what all the children call me."

"I think it's wonderful," I say. "Lib already adores you."

Betty smiles. "She invited me to come meet Long Long Peter. Said we could have a tea party with you and Mark and Weird Owl Yankovic."

"That's Libby," I say fondly. "Always the gracious hostess."

"She has excellent manners. You should be very proud."

I smile as I watch my daughter usher a smaller child in front of her in line, making sure he's steady on his feet before she takes her place. "I got pretty lucky."

"It's not luck. I work with kids for a living, and I know good parenting when I see it."

Something warm flickers in the center of my chest, surprising me with an accompanying pinprick of tears. I blink hard so Betty won't see. "Thank you."

She pats my arm and softens her voice. "Believe me, I know. It's hard being a single mom."

"Hardest thing I've ever done," I agree, overwhelmed by the urge to spill my guts to this woman I don't know at all.

But I do know her, in a way. We're both part of the struggling single moms club, even though we're at different stages of our membership. We know what it's like to question every choice we make, to wonder constantly if we're enough.

"It's rewarding, though," I add so she doesn't think I'm ungrateful. "Gratifying to know you can raise a child on your own without any help from anyone."

She nods thoughtfully. "I admire you," she says. "I'm not sure I could have done it without support from Cort and—well, from my other friends over the years."

I know from the way she says *friends* she means boyfriends. There, that's a tidbit Mark's shared with me, something I've squirreled away in my file of personal information. I touch Betty's hand, aware of the self-conscious note in her voice.

"I think maybe it's harder with boys," I say. "A friend of mine has two—nine and thirteen—and she's constantly worried about whether they've got enough male role models."

Betty's smile warms with appreciation. "That's true," she says. "You always worry you're not enough for them."

"I feel that way, too," I admit. "All the time. But at least with a daughter, I can relate. I remember how hard the social stuff is, and we can talk about being a girl and what kind of changes she'll go through as she gets older. If there's anything I don't know, I've got a whole tribe of girlfriends to be surrogate moms."

"It *is* different with boys." There's an unmistakable wistfulness in her voice. "I did my best with Mark, tried to give him role models where I could."

"You did an amazing job." I reach over and squeeze her hand. "He's a great guy, and he really admires you."

Tears glitter in the corners of her eyes. "Thank you, dear."

I let my gaze drift out over the ball pit, and I watch my daughter, my happy, well-adjusted, sweet daughter. How would she be different with a father figure in the picture?

My imagination floods with images of Mark and Libby together, discussing the merits of donuts or singing silly songs in the car. Longing, sharp and intense, pinches the center of my chest. I want that. I shouldn't, but I do, and I'm not sure how much longer I can fight it.

Betty's gone quiet beside me, and I try to think of something else I can share. Something to let her know I'm right there with her in questioning my choices as a single mom.

"I do sometimes worry how the whole paternity issue complicates things." I hesitate there, not sure how much Bree has shared about my situation, but positive Betty can relate on some level. "A kid deserves privacy, obviously, but there's a point where it's important to talk openly about the biological father and how—"

"Oh my God." Betty grips my arm, eyes wide as nickels, and she stares at me in amazement. "He told you." Her eyes fill with tears. "He loves you."

I watch her lip quiver as I try to make sense of what's happening. "What?"

The slow smile spreading over her face tells me these are happy tears, but I don't understand what I'm missing. "I'm almost positive you're the first person he's ever told," she says. "To be honest, I wasn't sure how much he knew. I always hoped Cort finally talked to him about it, but he never wanted to talk to *me*, so I just let him be."

There's a buzzing in the back of my brain, a nervous hum of uncertainty. I'm not even sure we're having the same conversation. "I don't—"

"Oh, sweetheart—I didn't mean to scare you." Her smile is so kind that I'm tempted to clam up. To just stand here basking in this motherly affection. "It's clear you feel the same way, or I wouldn't have said anything. I'm just so tickled you've cracked his armor."

She turns away and swipes at a tear that leaks from one eye. She's watching Libby now, trying to regain her composure while I try to figure out what the hell I've missed.

"Betty, I don't—" I stall out there, but she must hear something in my voice because she turns back to face me.

And then her smile falters. "Oh." She lifts a hand to her mouth. "Oh, dear."

"There's been a misunderstanding," I offer feebly, the understatement of the year.

"I thought—when you said—" Her brow furrows as she retraces her steps through our conversation. "You mentioned paternity questions. I just assumed Mark told you about Cort."

"No." I shake my head, wishing more than anything he had. That I didn't have to stand here facing his mother, acknowledging that I'm not as close to her son as she thought I was. As *I* thought I was.

A flicker of understanding sparks to a flame in the back of my brain. So there's a question about Mark's paternity? Okay, so...it happens. I mean, I guess I knew he had secrets, though this is a bigger one than a fear of spiders or an embarrassing childhood nickname.

Betty's still looking confused, so I hurry to explain. "Libby," I finally manage. "I was talking about Libby. I—we—we're dealing with some complicated paternity stuff with her right now, and I thought maybe you'd heard something from Bree or Mark or—"

"No." Betty shakes her head. "He hasn't said a word."

To either of us, sister.

I don't say that, of course, but it's dawning on me how much Mark's shut me out. How many chances he's had to open up to me, and how he's passed them up at every turn.

Betty's gaze shifts just over my shoulder and her face goes two shades paler. "Oh, no."

I pivot slowly, already knowing what I'm going to see. *Who* I'm going to see. How long has he been there, and what did he hear?

"Mark," Betty says, reaching for his arm as she looks up at his stony features. "Sweetheart, I think I may have just stepped in it."

"What?" He looks from her to me and back again, the crease deepening between his brows. "What are you talking about?"

"Paternity," I say softly, still not sure what's happening here. "Yours, apparently."

Slowly, one icy inch at a time, his expression turns to granite.

"I'm sorry," Betty says. "I thought you'd told her. Before he died, I thought your father would have—"

"No." Mark bites out that lone syllable less like the answer to a question and more like he's twisting the top onto a soda bottle threatening to fizz over. His jaw is clenched so tightly I see muscles twitching at his hairline.

Betty glances at me, then touches his arm again. "Do you want me to—"

"No," he says again, backing away as he rakes a hand through his hair. "I need to—I have to—*dammit.*"

He turns and lumbers away, hands clenched at his sides. I've never seen his shoulders bunched so tight.

"Go," Betty says, though she doesn't have to say it. I'm already moving after him. "He needs one of us, and I don't think it's me."

I'm not sure Mark needs anyone, or *wants* anyone at the moment, but when he looks over his shoulder and sees me, he slows his pace.

There's a moment of hesitation, and I swear I've seen it before. Not with Mark, but with deer on the side of the highway. That moment of choice, to turn and run back into the woods, or to leap out in front of an oncoming car.

He nods once. "Come on." He trudges away like a man headed to execution, expecting me to follow.

And of course, I do.

CHAPTER 18

MARK

Fuck, fuck, fuck.

The words pulse through my brain like a fight song as I thunder out of the arcade with the soft lilt of my mom and Chelsea's voices behind me.

My mom says something about watching Libby so we can talk, which is one more shred of evidence I'm an asshole. I didn't even think of that when I stomped off expecting Chelsea to follow.

I'm not thinking straight, what with all the clutter in my head. In an hour's time, I've gone from feeling like the luckiest son of a bitch in the world with a warm cluster of siblings and friends and community, to feeling pretty sure it's getting yanked out from under me like a shabby rug.

I reach the door of the supply closet and grab the handle with a shaky hand. "In here," I say as I wave my key card in front of it and push the door open.

If I were in my right mind, I'd head for a conference room or something. There are a zillion in the next building, but Chelsea doesn't complain as I hold the door open and usher her into a room filled with toilet paper rolls and cleaning supplies.

Further proof I'm the world's shittiest communicator. I can't even get the venue right.

"This is—um—nice." She fingers the sleeve of a cowgirl costume, one of dozens we bought for the cowpoke cookouts we do here as part of the kids' programs.

Libby would love it.

The thought flits through my brain before I stomp it under my boot. I can't afford to think that way. Not with Chelsea looking at me like she doesn't know who the fuck I am.

That makes two of us.

I drag a hand down my beard, trying to get my bearings. Trying to find a way to start this conversation. "What did my mom say?"

Chelsea doesn't flinch at the roughness of my words. "We don't have to do this now, Mark."

"Do what?"

"Talk about—whatever the hell you don't want to talk about." She chokes out a sad little laugh. "I don't even know."

"Why are you looking at me like that?" My voice cracks, and I hate myself even more. "Like you've never seen me before."

She hesitates. "Maybe I haven't. Not really. Maybe I've only seen what I wanted to."

Her words aren't accusing, that's the hell of it. They're cushioned with kindness and understanding, which I sure as fuck don't deserve.

I have no idea what to say to that. I stand there like an idiot, fists balled at my sides, wondering how the hell I've fucked this up so royally. How I can fix it.

Chelsea's still waiting, waiting for me to offer something. Anything that shows I can carry on a normal, adult conversation.

"We don't have to do this now," she says softly. "It's your birthday. A big one, right?"

I nod. That much I can offer. "Thirty," I tell her. "Today's my thirtieth birthday."

"Happy birthday," she says automatically.

There's a forced cheer to the words, but also a quiver. Hurt or anger, I'm not sure.

"It is a little strange, isn't it?" she continues, leaning back against a rack of paper towels like this is a normal conversation. Like there's anything about this that's normal. "We've been sleeping together for days—living under the same roof—and you didn't mention a milestone birthday?"

"I forgot." It sounds lame even to me, so I try again. "I don't like making a big deal."

"Okay." She's forcing as much brightness as she can into that one syllable. She wants to believe it. That's the hell of it, she wants to believe in me. "Seriously, Mark, it's fine. We don't have to do this now. I want you to have a good birthday."

I shake my head, knowing we're long past that. "What did my mother say?"

"Okay, we're doing this." She bites her lip, weighing her words. "Something about questionable paternity." She laughs, but it's a hollow, brittle sound. "I thought at first she was talking about Libby. That you'd told her something or—"

"I wouldn't," I tell her. "I'd never breathe a word to anyone."

Tears flood her eyes, and she nods. "I know you wouldn't," she says. "That's exactly it. You're like a steel door with the hinges welded shut."

I don't think that's a compliment.

"Look, Chelsea," I begin, but then I stop myself. What can I tell her that won't send her running the other way, convinced I'm a fraud or a failure or a misfit or—

"Tell me, Mark." Her eyes are pleading, her voice shaky. "Tell me something, *anything* real. Let me in."

Jesus Christ, that's the scariest thing I've ever heard. I don't know what to say so I say nothing at all, which isn't helping. Not a damn bit.

She waits a long damn time. Longer than I deserve. When she

speaks again, her voice is so soft I can hardly hear. "I've let you into the most private, guarded rooms of my life," she says. "Doors I've never opened for anyone, ever. But I'm still standing here on your front porch with my breath fogging up the glass, just peering through the window because you won't let me in at all. Not even a little bit."

"I—don't know where to start."

"Start anywhere. Your life, your scars, whatever the story is with your father."

I close my eyes, playing it out in my mind. Once I say the words out loud, it's all over. It becomes real, and my whole world unravels.

I'm not Cort Bracelyn's son.

Which means I'm not Bree's brother, not Sean's brother or James's or Jonathan's. I'm not anyone at all, not a part of this resort or a part of this family or this life I've managed to build for myself.

I'm no one.

I open my eyes to find Chelsea watching me.

The words scrape their way up my throat like barbed hooks. "I can't."

She jerks back like I've thrown two bricks at her, one after the other.

I. Can't.

She looks me in the eyes for a long time. "I see."

When she drops her gaze, I know that's a bad sign. "I guess I'm the idiot," she says, shaking her head. "I'm the one who thought this was different. Who thought *you* were different because you had so much to offer. Affection. Protection. The kind of strength and selflessness I've only dreamed of."

"But that's not enough."

Her throat moves as she swallows. "Not if you're just going through the motions. If I'm offering you my heart and soul and all my darkest secrets, and you're offering me a shield. It's wonderful, it's noble, God knows I appreciate it—but it's not enough. Not for me."

Say it.

Tell her you love her.

Tell her what you're afraid of.

But my tongue lays frozen in my mouth, unable to form the words. Unable to figure out who the fuck I even am. I'm standing on the edge of a cliff that I've known all along was probably there, shrouded in mist and thick nets of moss. I pretended it wasn't there, but I always knew, and it would be so damn easy to jump right over the edge. To grab Chelsea's hand and trust love to be our fucking parachute.

I'm not who you think I am.

I'm not who anyone thinks I am.

I'm not a Bracelyn.

I don't belong.

I can't say it. I can't let it be real.

"I'm going to go now." Her voice is soft, her steps even softer as she moves backward toward the door. "When you decide you're ready to let someone in, give me a call."

My hands ball into fists, and I close my eyes, willing myself to say something, anything.

But as the door clicks shut behind her, I know I've made a choice.

And she's made hers.

CHAPTER 19

CHELSEA

Mark's mother takes one look at my face when I emerge from the supply closet and presses her lips together. "Go," she says softly. "I've got her."

Maybe it's single mom intuition, but she seems to know I need a moment alone. That I'm seconds away from falling apart, and the last thing I need is for Libby to witness it.

I glance at the ball pit and see Libby's playing happily with her new friend, both girls swimming through a sea of red and blue and green plastic bubbles. She's laughing like the world is a perfect, rainbow-hued utopia, and for her, it is. I want it to stay that way as long as possible.

So I go, murmuring a promise to be back in an hour. I just need some air, a few moments of quiet to figure out how the hell I've managed to do this again. To press myself magnetlike to a man hellbent on pushing me away.

I burst through the side door and out into the darkness. No one follows, especially not Mark. Cloaked in darkness, I skirt past the ballroom where the party's still in full swing. There's Senator Grassnab, deep in conversation with Austin on the far side of the room. Neither looks up to notice me scuttling through the shadows, making my way to the other side of the resort.

I'm not even sure where I'm going until the glow of the main lodge flickers into view. The dining room is bright as a lantern, with dinner rush in full swing. I jog around to the other side, making a beeline for the pastry kitchen. Thank God Sean told me about it. Maybe he knew I'd need the therapy at some point. For as long as I can recall, baking has been my solace, my comfort, my safe place.

I've never needed it more.

Pushing through the side door, I move down the hallway by the restrooms and head for the nondescript door at the back. My hands are shaking as I pull my key card out of my pocket and wave it in front of the scanner. It clicks open like a welcome, a wave of cinnamon and vanilla greeting me warmly.

My sleeve tangles on the door handle, and I waste a few precious minutes struggling to free myself. Tears drip down my face, blurring my vision and making me feel like an even bigger idiot than I already did.

God. Finally, I'm in, safe in the spice-scented cocoon. Here, I can pretend for just a few minutes that I haven't screwed up again. That I didn't fling myself head first into another relationship with a guy unwilling to offer more than a flimsy paper cutout of himself.

I make my way to the sink in the corner and wash my hands, stopping to splash water on my face. It'll be okay. Everything will be fine; I can get through this.

Spotting a row of chef's aprons on pegs along the wall, I pull one down and cinch it around my waist. Then I get to work.

Poking my head in the cooler, I locate the tools required to soothe my soul. Butter, eggs, fresh milk from the dairy down the road. I drag them out and pile them on the stainless-steel counter beside tidy canisters of flour and sugar.

I don't even know what I'm making, but my hands are flying, going through the motions on autopilot.

Just like Mark.

No. I push the thoughts aside, forcing myself to get lost in the familiar comforts of sifting, stirring, mixing.

But my mind won't be easily subdued.

How did I not know? How did I miss the fact that I'd thrown myself face first into an ocean of caring and commitment, while Mark stood coolly on the shore, not daring to wade in?

I thought I knew him. I wasn't dumb enough to think I'd burrowed all the way inside the warm chambers of that big, cavernous heart of his, but I thought I'd at least touched the surface.

But it turns out I wasn't close. Not even a little.

Flour sifts through my fingers like fairy dust, and I lose track of time. How long do I work like that? Five minutes, ten, cracking eggs and stirring in cocoa powder until my heart rate starts to slow.

Click.

My head snaps up at the sound, but it takes my eyes a moment to adjust. When they do, my brain synapses fire in a fizzy repeat of *what the hell*?

A woman, cloaked in a slinky black dress, stands by the doorway with a thick gold bangle on one arm. Her smile is a brittle slash of red lipstick and perfect white teeth, and her sleek blond bob glows bright under the kitchen lights.

I notice these things in sequence, cataloguing them one by one—dress, jewelry, makeup, hair—with the growing awareness that I'm avoiding the one thing in this pretty picture that chills me to the bone.

A pistol, gripped in her manicured hand, pointed right at my head.

CHAPTER 20

MARK

I try to go back to the party after Chelsea flees the closet. It's my damn birthday after all, and they went to so much trouble.

I stand outside for a long time, looking through the windows like a kid outside the candy shop with no quarters in my pocket to buy gummy bears.

Bree's bustling around talking to people, the perfect hostess with a champagne flute in one hand. She glances at her watch, then says something to Jonathan. His brows crease, and he gives a quick shrug.

They'll forget eventually. My absence from the party, my absence from the next board meeting or the one after that. Like plucking a weed from a flower bed, no one will miss what didn't belong in the first place.

Sean moves past the window with a platter of the chocolate-dipped strawberries, but he doesn't see me standing outside. He knows those are my favorite, and my big, dumb heart fills with a longing that has nothing to do with sweets.

Goddammit.

I grew up an only child. I've been independent my whole life, so how the hell did I get so attached to these late-in-life siblings?

But I'm not one of them, I never have been, and it's only a matter of time before they know it.

Austin moves past the window, sticking to Senator Assgrab like flypaper. Good, that's one less thing to worry about as far as Chelsea's concerned. He mentioned something in passing earlier tonight, a comment about suspicious banking activity that has the boys in blue watching every move the Senator's making. So that's a relief. With any luck, Chelsea's drama will be over soon, and she can go back to her normal life.

A life that doesn't include me.

The thought feels like a flaming boot to the chest.

"Is there a reason you're spying on your own birthday party?"

I jump about ten feet in the air, no small feat for a guy my size. Whirling around, I come face to face with James. He's got his hands in his pockets, tie perfectly straight, and he's leaning against the side of the building like it's cocktail hour at the fucking country club.

"What the fuck are you doing out here?"

"Stepped outside to take a phone call," he says, unperturbed by my language. Or by anything, really. "Nice evening, isn't it?"

His expression is neutral, no flicker of emotion at all. I remember our father sometimes called him Iceman Bracelyn, a reference to James's courtroom demeanor, or maybe just his personality.

Then I remember Cort Bracelyn is probably not my dad, and James is probably not my brother, and I hate myself all over again. "Fuck."

James doesn't flinch. Just looks at me with those cool, green eyes, assessing me like I'm a legal brief.

"So," he finally says. "Are you going to ask me?"

"Ask you what?"

"I ran into your mother."

I frown, not following the conversation. "Are you high?"

James doesn't dignify that with a response. Just pins me with the world's iciest green eyes, Bracelyn eyes, but colder. "I was the executor of Dad's will," he says. "You know that, right?"

I'm still not following, so I do what I always do when I feel thrown off-balance. "Why the fuck should I care?"

He sighs like he's bored with the conversation. "I'm not telling you to be smug. I'm telling you because Dad entrusted me with a lot of documentation. Paperwork, files, information he thought might be of interest to the family at some point."

There's a slow prickling of hair on the back of my neck. Like my lizard brain figures something out before the rest of me catches up.

"Paternity tests?" I guess.

He nods. "Among other things."

All the air leaves my lungs. I stand there like a deflated balloon, like the biggest loser who ever lived. "So, you know."

James crosses one ankle over the other, still leaning against the side of the building. "I know the truth," he says. "Do you want to?"

No.

Everything inside me screams that word, howls it while clinging to the last fading memories of my childhood. The baseball playoffs where Dad came and sat there in the front row, chest puffed up as he told the guy next to him how the big kid who'd just stolen home was his son. *His son.*

Or the summer I visited after high school when I told him I might not go to college, and he looked me dead in the eye and said, "you're going to fucking college if I have to drag you there myself and pay someone a hundred grand a day to hold your sorry ass in that chair and pour the education into your ear with a funnel."

Yeah, he wasn't a touchy-feely dad. He wasn't even a very

good one, but he was mine. The only father I've ever known, my only link to this family.

Until now.

I don't know what James sees on my face, but I know I haven't mastered the impassive thing like he has. Not even close.

"Let me ask you this," he says, pushing off the side of the building and taking a step closer. "Your girlfriend, Chelsea—what happens if the condom breaks?"

"Jesus." Not what I was expecting him to say. "I'm not discussing my sex life with you."

James snorts with disgust. "I'm not asking about your sex life," he says with exaggerated patience. "And this is also not a moral discussion about right to life or a woman's right to choose."

"What the fuck is it then?"

"I watched you the other night with Libby," he says. "And I have a hard time believing that if a biological child came along—one who had your DNA, your eyes, your nose, your thick fucking skull—that you'd love that child any less than one who's not genetically yours."

I stare at my brother. I stare at him for a long, long time, so long I can sense him getting uncomfortable.

"I'm going to ask you again," he says. "Are you ready to know? Not guess, not wonder, not bury your head in the sand like a fucking coward—are you ready to actually *know*?"

The choice is mine.

The second shitty choice I've had to make in the last hour, and I already know I fucked up the first one. I knew it the instant Chelsea walked out of that closet, and I felt a giant fucking hole rip open in the center of my chest.

I've spent the first thirty years of my life as Cort Bracelyn's son. I pushed aside my suspicions because I wanted to be that guy. I wanted it so badly that I wove it into my identity tight enough that I could no longer tell where reality stopped and my childish wishes began.

But I know it's time to yank the thread.

It stings like hell to think of losing all of it—son, brother, family member—but there's something else that hurts more.

Losing Chelsea. Losing Libby. Losing the guy I am when I'm with them. That right there, that's the only truth that matters.

"I want to know," I tell him. "I'm ready to know."

He nods, unsurprised by my answer. "Follow me."

He turns toward the lodge, headed for the side with the administrative offices. I lumber after him, trying not to drag my feet. This is it, my final breaths as a guy who doesn't know for sure. After this, it'll all be on the table. No more sitting hunched in the fucking corner with my hands over my ears and my eyes squeezed tightly shut.

James leads me across the lawn and through a side door into his cavernous office. He flips the lights on and gestures to a chair. "Have a seat."

I do what he says, wondering if these will be our last words to each other as brothers. I stare at the back of his head as he unlocks a file cabinet and pulls out a green folder. I say the words to his back because I sure as fuck can't say them to his face.

"You've been a good brother."

He stiffens but says nothing. He doesn't turn around, either, so I keep going. "Whatever's in there, no matter what it says, it's meant everything being part of this family."

He turns around slowly, green eyes blazing. He stares at me with his jaw clenched tight. "You are the biggest dumb shit."

I blink. "Excuse me?"

James shakes his head and drops into his chair. "Of all the lame-ass, stupid, presumptuous—"

"And people think *I'm* the insensitive asshole brother?"

He shoves the file at me in disgust. "Open it."

I hesitate, hand on the cover. Then I take a deep breath and flip it open.

My dad's handwriting is the first thing I notice. It's a letter, one page, on lined notebook paper. I stare at the sharp spikes of the M, the blunt edges of the K, committing this moment to memory.

And then I start to read.

Dear Mark,

If you're reading this, two things have happened: I'm dead, and you decided for some lame-ass, dumbshit reason, probably spewed at you by your batshit mother, that you want to know if I'm your fucking father.

I look up at James. "I'm definitely feeling the love."

He doesn't smile. "Keep reading."

I lower my gaze and continue.

From the day your mother told me she was knocked up, I never questioned if you were mine. Sure, there were plenty of other dicks in the picture, your mom was hot as fuck and—

"I'm not sure I want to read this." I look to James for assurance, but he's sitting with crossed hands on top of his head and a cool, impassive expression.

"Keep going."

Bossy asshole.

I sigh and lower my gaze again, skimming as best as I can over the part about my mother's skills in the sack. There are some things a guy can't unsee.

I always knew it might not be me who slipped one past the goalie. But I also knew it didn't matter. You were my kid before you took your first breath, before you shit your first diaper or lost your first tooth or got your first BJ. You were always my kid, which is why I tore up the stupid fucking paternity test your mother insisted on getting.

But I'm getting older and there might come a time when you give a shit. Maybe you're wondering about family history of insanity or maybe you need to figure out your genetic risk of ass cancer. Whatever. I got another copy of the test. If James has done his job, he's handing it to you right now, and it's up to you whether to open it. It's up to you to believe that no matter what it says, you'll always be my fucking kid.

Dad

NOT "LOVE, DAD" or "Affectionately yours," which is further proof he really wrote this. Not that I needed it. The words are all Cort Bracelyn. I stare at the letter, breathing in and out, until James speaks.

"Here," he says. "Take it."

I look up at the sealed envelope he holds like an offering. I reach for it with a shaking hand, but James pulls it back.

"No matter what it says, you're my brother," he says. "Get that through your thick fucking skull."

A lump balls up in my throat, thick and hot. "You already know what's in here?"

"Yes."

"How long?" I ask. "How long have you known?"

"Seven years," he says. "Dad named me executor when I graduated from law school."

I swallow hard, trying to digest that. "Way before he died. Way before we started this place."

"Yep."

I grab for the envelope again, and this time he lets me. His face is impassive as I tear it open and unfold the paper inside. As the words start to blur, I force myself to make sense of them.

"Mother," "child," "alleged father," all the columns blur together in a haze of alphabet soup.

When I look up, James is still watching me. "Any questions?"

"So, he wasn't my father."

"He was," James says. "You just don't have his DNA."

I breathe in and out a few times, testing my lungs to see if they feel different. If my body is still the same. It is and it isn't, but there's a lightness in my shoulders that wasn't there before.

As far as I can tell, the world hasn't ended.

"It's your choice whether to tell the others," he says. "If you choose not to, I'll take the secret to my grave."

"And if I choose to tell?"

"I'd stake my job on the fact that it won't change a damn thing. Not for any of us."

The words touch me unexpectedly. Nothing in James's world matters more than his job, so he must be pretty confident.

"I'll tell them," I say, positive it's the right thing to do. "No more secrets."

I'm not talking about the DNA shit, though that goes without saying. I'm going to tell Bree and Sean and Jonathan, and even if it does change things, I'm willing to live with that.

But it's Chelsea I'm thinking about. Chelsea who deserves the whole truth, the whole me. She always deserved that, and I was too damn scared to realize.

"There's one more thing." James presses his palms to the desk as he stands, turning to open a cupboard behind him. There's a safe inside, something I never noticed before. Not that I spend much time rifling through my brother's shit.

My brother.

I roll the word around in my brain, trying to decide if it feels any different now that I know. It feels more like a marble and less like a sharp-edged burr, and I think maybe that's a good thing.

"This is for you." He pulls out a cigar box and hands it to me.

Cohiba Behike. I know from being around Cort Bracelyn that these run $18,000 a box.

And I know from seeing this same box in my mother's closet —and from being a nosy little shit—what's inside.

I flip it open to be sure, hinges creaking as I trace my thumb over the familiar ding in the corner. I stare at the contents, then flip the lid shut and look at James.

"You're not going to read that note?" he asks.

"Later," I tell him, handing the box back to him. "There's something more urgent I need to do."

He nods and turns to slide the box back in the safe. When he turns back around, I'm already halfway to the door.

"Go get your girl," he says, smiling for the first time this evening. "I have faith in you, brother."

CHAPTER 21

CHELSEA

I take a deep breath and stare at the pistol.

Yep, it's a gun all right, shiny and big and definitely capable of blowing a great big hole in my body.

As I lift my eyes to the woman's face, there's a flicker of recognition in the back of my brain. "Mrs. Grassnab," I say. "Are you lost?"

"Don't be cute with me, you little homewrecker."

I grip the edge of the counter, fighting to stay upright and not to pee myself in terror. Holy crap, this is really happening.

"Mrs. Grassnab." My voice shakes, but I keep my composure. To do what it takes to keep myself alive and un-shot. "I think there's been a misunderstanding. If you'll just put the gun down—"

"There's no misunderstanding," she says. "I'm tying up loose ends."

Her glossy blond hair slips over one eye, and she blows it off her forehead, never once lowering the gun. I keep my eyes fixed on her face, not daring to glance at the pistol.

"My husband is a serious contender to be President of the United States," she says. "If you think for one second, I'm going to let that be derailed by some floozy coming forward with a scandalous love child—"

"I'd never do that," I insist. It might not be smart to argue with a woman holding a gun, but Libby is *no one's* scandalous love child.

"So, you don't deny it."

Crap. Was I supposed to? This is my first negotiation with a crazed person pointing a pistol at me, so I don't know the rules.

I lick my lips and fight to stay calm. "Look, Libby is six," I tell her. "The world's sweetest, most gentle, generous little girl."

"Who looks remarkably like my husband," she says. "I had suspicions a few years ago, so I looked you up. I had you followed; I even watched you at the playground."

Dear God, the woman is nuts.

Like I hadn't already figured that out, but it's clearer now.

She keeps going, since I can't seem to find words of my own. "I thought at first I could scare you out of town," she says. "Terrorize you into keeping your trap shut for good. But then you hooked up with the resort people, and it's pretty clear you're not going anywhere. You found your meal ticket, didn't you?"

I force myself not to react. There's no point sinking to her level. "I'd never breathe a word to anyone," I tell her. "Doesn't it mean something that I've kept my mouth shut? I've never asked for child support or even breathed a word to Wal—to Senator Grassnab."

The flash of fury in her eyes tells me I'd be smart not to give her any reminders that I've been intimate with her husband. The memory of it sends a shudder of shame through me.

One more reminder of my horrible judgement with men.

"He doesn't know," she says simply. "About your daughter or about this little—complication. Sometimes a woman has to take matters into her own hands."

Maybe I can play off her motherly sympathies. I'm a mom, she's a mom, we have that in common. "My daughter needs me,

Mrs. Grassnab," I tell her. "Just like your children need you. Please."

Fire blazes in her eyes. "You've met my children?"

"No! Absolutely not." God, maybe it's better if I don't speak. Keeping my eyes fixed on her, I scan the room with my peripheral vision. There's a block of knives over by the window, but that won't do me much good from here.

"Please, Mrs. Grassnab," I urge. "Put the gun down. We can pretend this never happened."

She gives a bitter little snort. "Hardly. People come out of the woodwork all the time the higher someone climbs on the political ladder. I should have nipped this in the bud a long time ago."

I glance at the weapon, which is definitely still a gun, and definitely still pointed at me. Swallowing back my fear, I try a different tack. "The police chief is in the next building," I tell her. "He's a friend of mine. The kind of guy who'd notice things like gunfire and bleeding bodies in the kitchen."

"There won't be any blood," she says matter-of-factly. "I've thought this through."

"Of course you have." Just what the world needs, thoughtful murderers.

"If we do this right, there will be an unfortunate little kitchen incident," she says. "A sink full of water, an electrical appliance, a—"

Boom!

I hit the floor, not certain what's happened, but pretty sure ducking is the best move when a gun goes off. Covering my head with my hands, I look down at my body. No holes that I can see, and since my eyeballs work, I trust they're still in my head, which is still attached to my body. All good signs.

"I'll take that."

Mark!

I snap my head up to see him plucking the pistol from Mrs. Grassnab's hand like it's a toy. The scent of gunpowder hangs thick in the air, but no one appears to be shot. She's rubbing the side of her head where the door must have hit her, too stunned to protest.

"Give that back!" she demands. "Who the hell do you think you are?"

He ignores her and rushes forward to help me to my feet. "Are you okay?" His hand is firm and strong, and he lifts me like I weigh nothing.

"I'm fine," I breathe, flinching as he whips the gun around to point it at Mrs. Grassnab.

"You," he says. "Don't move."

She puts her hands in the air, eyeing him up and down. "I think there's been a misunderstanding—"

"Oh, *now* there's a misunderstanding?" My fury bubbles to the surface now that I don't need to play polite anymore. "This psycho tried to kill me."

Mark's whole body is rigid, all six feet five inches of him. I've never seen him so furious. "You tried to kill my girlfriend."

Mrs. Grassnab does her best to offer a *who, me?* look. "Don't be ridiculous. I just came in here looking for the ladies' room."

I snort out loud. "With a handgun?"

"I wasn't talking to you," she says, flipping her hair. "If you'll just put the gun down and stop looking all menacing, we can talk about this like sane, rational—"

"I've had enough of you." Mark's voice is surprisingly calm as he sets the gun on the counter. He gives it a distasteful glance, or maybe that's for Mrs. Grassnab. Before she can make a run for it, he grabs her by the wrist and pulls her toward the wall with the aprons.

She sputters, stumbling in her high heels. "What are you—"

"I need you to sit still and shut up for a minute," Mark says, yanking an apron off the pegs and making quick work of lacing the strings around her wrists. "I have something important I need to say, and it can't wait."

She sputters again as Mark cinches the apron strings tight behind her back. "If you have something to say to me—"

"Not to you," he snaps, exasperation turning his voice into a growl. "To her. The woman I *love,* dammit."

Wait, what?

He looks at me and frowns. "This isn't how I saw this going."

"It's okay," I tell him. "We can start over."

He nods, gaze sweeping over my body. "You're sure you're okay?"

"Positive." Did he say he loves me?

He steps forward and takes my hands in his. "Chelsea, I love you. I love you so damn much it scared the shit out of me, and I acted like an asshole."

Behind him, Mrs. Grassnab scoffs. "This sounds like victim blaming. I was a therapist for years. No one *makes* you act like—"

"Shut up," I snap, keeping my eyes on Mark. "You love me?"

"More than anything," he says, squeezing my hands. "I've been afraid to open up because I wasn't sure you'd like who I really was if I told you. I wasn't sure *I'd* like myself, or even who I really was without—*God,* I'm botching this."

"You definitely should have practiced," Mrs. Grassnab observes. "You only get one chance to tell a woman that you—"

"Shut up!" Mark and I bark the words in unison, hands still linked together.

Mark squeezes mine and keeps going. "I'm not a real Bracelyn," he says. "Not by blood, anyway, but I've realized it doesn't matter. A name or a bloodline doesn't make me who I am. And the guy I am when I'm with you is the best version of me I can be."

"Oh, Mark," I say, tears clouding my eyes. "I love you no matter what's in your DNA. I love you for the guy you are, and there's nothing you could tell me about yourself that would make me love you less."

"Try having him tell you he's been boffing bimbos on the

side," Mrs. Grassnab scoffs. "See how everlasting that affection is when he brings home chlamydia for the third t—"

"Shut. Up." Mark glares at her, and this time, Mrs. Grassnab zips it.

He turns back to me, fingers still laced through mine. "I don't know what's going to happen with this resort or my family or any of this DNA stuff. But I know that no matter what, I choose you."

A tear slips down my cheek, and I dash it away with my shoulder, not wanting to pull my hands from his. "I choose you, too. Always."

"God, Chelss." He pulls me tight against him, wrapping me in the biggest, warmest, strongest hug of my life. "I promise to let you in," he murmurs into my hair. "I'll tell you anything you want to know. Anything at all."

"We've got time," I tell him. "All the time in the world."

He draws back, remembering our audience. "Speaking of time, someone's going to be serving some."

I frown at Mrs. Grassnab. "We should probably call the police."'

"Won't be necessary." The door swings open and Austin strides into the kitchen. He's flanked by Officers Studebaker and Leopold, both of whom have their guns drawn. "We tend to be summoned by gunfire."

"Austin," I breathe. "Is Libby—"

"Safe and sound and back at Mark's cabin with Betty," he says. He takes a step toward Mrs. Grassnab, nodding with approval at the apron-string handcuffs. "Very nice," he says. "Your husband is on his way to the station right now. We've got questions for both of you."

She mutters a string of unladylike curse words as Officers Studebaker and Leopold each take her by an arm and lead her out of the pastry kitchen.

Austin watches them go, then turns back to me. "We'll have

questions for you, too, but you're free to go back to your cabin," he says. "It could be a late night."

"Not a problem," Mark says, slinging an arm around me and pulling me close. "We've got lots to talk about."

"We do?"

He nods. "Open, honest, no-bullshit, no-holds-barred, vulnerable as fuck conversation."

"Oh."

"From me," he says, in case that wasn't obvious. "I want to tell you everything, Chelss. I want to let you in. I don't know what the hell I was so afraid of before, but I'm ready to let you see the real me." His throat moves as he swallows, and he looks unsure for the first time. "If you still want me."

"God." I throw my arms around him and squeeze him tight. "I still want you. More than ever. More than anything."

"Good," he says, squeezing me back. "Then let's do it."

EPILOGUE

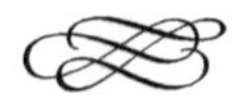

MARK

"Thanks for coming." I follow Bree and Austin through my living room as they gather their things and say their goodbyes. "Aren't you forgetting something?"

Austin turns back and whistles for his dog. Virginia Woof thumps her tail on my carpet but doesn't take her focus off the task of cleaning Long Long Peter's ears. Between that and the fact that Libby is rubbing the dog's belly, Virginia's in heaven and not looking to leave anytime soon.

"She can sleep over if you want," Chelsea offers. "I'll have Libby bring her by in the morning."

Libby bounces with energy, her birthday hat slipping sideways on her head. "Please? Oh, please, Aunt Bree?"

Bree smiles and slides her arm around Austin's waist. "We probably can't say no to the birthday girl. It's in the manual or something."

"Just don't feed her any cupcakes," Austin says. "She passed gas for three days last time."

Libby dissolves into a puddle of giggles, because farting is funny to a seven-year-old no matter who's doing it. "Thanks, Uncle Austin."

Aunt Bree. Uncle Austin.

There's no blood relation among any of us here, save Libby and Chelsea. None of us are married yet, either, which I guess is a damn good reminder that family has nothing to do with blood ties or wedding vows or any of that shit. It has everything to do with who you decide to love with your whole damn heart and hold tight to no matter what.

"By the way," Bree says, hesitating in the doorway. "I'm not really one for those cheesy social media announcements or some huge proclamation at a family gathering, so I'll just tell you now—"

"Oh my God." Chelsea draws a hand to her mouth. "You're—"

"Yep." Bree grins.

"For sure?"

"For sure."

Austin gets a big dopey grin and puts his hand on Bree's back. "We've known a few weeks."

I look from Chelsea to Bree to Austin and wonder what the fuck everyone's talking about. "Will someone please translate this conversation?"

Chelsea laughs as she pulls my sister in for a hug. That's when I notice Bree's touching her belly. Pretty sure it's not because she ate too many cupcakes.

"Holy crap," I say. "You're knocked up?"

"I am." My sister is glowing, and she laughs as I take my turn hugging her. "Kinda doing it in reverse order. We'll have a quiet wedding, maybe in the next month or so."

"Congratulations," I tell her, turning to shake Austin's hand. "Way to go."

"Thanks."

I'm half tempted to salute or something, but I settle for glancing back toward the living room. Libby's too far away and too wrapped up in playing with her birthday gifts to care what the grownups are talking about, which is just as well. No sense overshadowing her birthday with news of some other baby's impending arrival.

"Congratulations," Chelsea says. "We're so happy for you."

I love that she speaks for both of us. Chelsea and me, a unit, a *family*. My big, dumb heart swells like a mylar balloon.

"Thanks for having us over," Bree says, then peers around me to shout back to Libby. "Happy birthday, kiddo!"

"Thanks!" Lib shouts back. "G'night."

Chelsea gives a big, contented sigh as the door clicks shut behind Bree and Austin. She turns to me and smiles. "Well, that was amazing."

"Yeah." I'm grinning like a dumbass, so happy for my sister.

But that's not the only thing I'm jazzed about right now.

I watch as Chelsea moves back through the living room, and I admire the sway of her hips as I trail after her.

"Was the party everything you wanted it to be, Lib?" she asks.

"It was the best party *ever*," she says. "My friends thought the horses were cool, and I love Grandma Bootie's present."

Long Long Peter was less enthusiastic about the sweater my mother knitted for him, but he doesn't seem to be suffering much as he rolls to his side so Virginia Woof can clean his other ear.

"And I like the stuffie she brought me, too," Libby says. "The giraffe sheep."

"Llama," Chelsea reminds her, even though "giraffe sheep" is so fucking adorable we almost didn't correct her.

"Yes," Libby agrees. "I'm naming him Llamanade."

"Perfect," I say, clearing my throat. "There's one more present."

Chelsea's head tilts in confusion, and she leans close for one of those low-volume parental conferences I'm just now learning are a thing. "Am I forgetting something we got her?" she whispers.

Nope, she's not. This one's a surprise for both of them, and I'm nervous as hell about it. Nervous, but also excited.

"Have a seat," I say, gesturing to the couch. "Both of you, right next to each other."

Mother and daughter exchange a look of intrigue as they settle themselves on the sofa side by side. Libby's pigtails are crooked, and her face is smeared with chocolate, while Chelsea's decked out in leggings and one of my old shirts.

"I turn into a pumpkin after nine," she told me earlier after Libby's friends got picked up, and the party was just down to family. "Might as well be comfortable."

"You're beautiful when you're comfortable," I told her, kissing her as she rolled up the sleeves on my old plaid flannel.

As I look at them now—both of my girls—I'm pretty damn sure I've never seen so much beautiful in one place. Not even the cupcake displays at Chelsea's shop, which is saying something.

I settle on the edge of the coffee table I built from an old Ponderosa pine that got hit by lightning last fall. It's scarred and sturdy and my favorite piece of furniture in the whole house.

Taking a deep breath, I begin. "Libby and Chelsea." My voice wobbles a little, so I clear my throat. "The two of you have become the most important people in my whole life. Every day, you make me smile and laugh, and I love the crap out of both of you."

Libby giggles, delighted by the curse word as all good seven-year-olds are. That's another thing I've learned lately: A curse word or two never killed any kid, and it's okay to cut myself some slack.

Chelsea's smiling, but there's still a question in her eyes. I wonder if she knows what's coming. If she recognizes an even bigger question I'm trying to get out in my own fumbly way.

"You are my family," I say to my girls. "Both of you, unquestionably, until the day I keel over from sugar overdose, you're my reason for getting out of bed in the morning and the reason I want to get into it at night." I nod at Libby. "That part's more for your mom."

She grins. "I figured."

"But tucking you in at night is one of my favorite parts of every day."

"Because Alice the Camel," she says.

"Yeah." But that's only a tiny fraction of why, and I hope she knows it.

"You're our family, too," Libby says. "Right, Mom?"

"Absolutely." Chelsea reaches out to touch my hand, which I didn't realize is shaking.

There's a damn lump in my throat, too, so I swallow it back and keep going. "So, we're all each other's family," I continue. "And if it's okay with both of you, I'd like to make that official."

I reach down beside me and pull open the drawer I built into the coffee table. Inside is the cigar box James has been keeping for me in his safe. I pull it out and rest it on my knees.

Libby cocks her head. "I'm old enough to smoke cigars now?"

"Definitely not." I fight the urge to smile. This is serious stuff, right? "There's something in here that belonged to my father. And before he had them, they belonged to his mom—my grandma."

I'm leaving out a few details, though I'll explain later to Chelsea. I'll tell her how my dad had an endless supply of valuable gemstones, courtesy of his mother's extensive collection and her willingness to fork over a handful any time my father felt like proposing to someone.

He got that urge a lot, but that's beside the point.

"Two times, my dad proposed to Grandma Bootie," I explain as I extract the first ring box. "And both times, she said no."

Pretty sure the rings had nothing to do with her answer, or with why she eventually returned them both to my dad. Just in case there's any lingering bad juju, I had them melted down and the gemstones reset into something new. Something just for the three of us, the family I'm hoping we'll become.

"Oh, Mark." Chelsea's eyes glitter with tears as I open the first box to reveal a tiny gold pendant studded with sapphires. Blue, Libby's favorite color, and I hold it out as her eyes get bigger.

"Giving you a ring felt sorta creepy, but you're part of this proposal, and I wanted you to have something." I slide to one knee, taking the necklace out of the box. "Libby, would it be okay if I asked your mom to marry me? If I promised to be your stepdad forever and ever, and to love you even more than your mom's gingerbread cupcakes with candied orange and molasses?"

Libby laughs, pigtails swaying as she nods. "Yes!" she says, bouncing a little as I clasp the necklace for her. "I say yes. I love you, Mark."

I half expected questions about what stepdad means, but she's paid attention. We've talked a lot these last couple months about families and how they all look different. She's only recently learned about her biological father, and how he's chosen not to be involved.

We're probably a few years away from the more detailed explanation that includes details like Senator Assgrab's wife in prison for attempted murder, or how he halted his presidential run to focus on family matters. She's also too young to hear how I've chosen not to learn about *my* biological father. Maybe someday we'll get there, Libby and me, to a point we're ready to make those connections. But right now, there's no rush.

I take another deep breath and turn to face the woman I love more than anyone else in the world. The woman who just wiped her eyes on the sleeve of my faded plaid shirt.

"Chelsea." The wobble is back in my voice, but she doesn't seem to care. She's smiling her biggest, broadest smile, and it's enough to keep me going. "I've loved you from the first moment you stood there in your stripey apron feeding me cupcakes," I tell her. "But back then, I was too dumb and too scared to recognize love when it hit me upside the head like an axe."

I pull out the second jeweler's box and open it, and she gasps.

I think it's a good gasp, but I can't tell with her covering her mouth like that.

"Oh my God, Mark! It's so beautiful." She's flat-out sobbing now, tears rolling down her face as she laughs and smiles and displays a bunch of other emotions I'm still learning to recognize.

"My mom helped come up with the design," I tell her. "She said tungsten's one of the toughest metals, and diamonds are one of the toughest stones, and all that strength put together makes something beautiful. Something like you. Like us."

I slip the ring from the box, admiring how the rose gold inlay matches the glints of red in her hair. It's beautiful, but the woman whose finger I'm slipping it on puts the damn ring to shame.

It flashes as she holds her finger up, laughing and crying and hugging me and Libby in a great, big, soggy, laughter-filled embrace.

"Wait," I say, pulling back a little. "Was I supposed to wait for a yes before shoving that on your finger?"

She laughs and wipes her eyes. "I don't recall hearing a question."

Oh, shit. I forgot that part, didn't I?

Well, nothing about this family, this union, has gone according to the rule book. Why would the proposal be any different?

"Will you marry me, Chelsea?" I ask. "Make me the happiest man who ever lived, which you've already done, but now it'll be official."

"Yes," she says, laughing as she touches the side of my face. "Yes, absolutely."

This time it's me pulling her in for a hug, her and Libby all at once. I wrap my arms around both of them, sealing us into a big, warm cocoon of love and family and togetherness.

"Did I do okay?" I ask. "The proposal, the jewelry, all that stuff? It's the first time I've ever done that."

Chelsea laughs and pulls back to look in my eyes. "It was perfect," she says. "A first time and a last time all rolled into one."

Libby wiggles between us. "And a happily ever after."

"Exactly."

***

Ready for James and Lily's story? That's next in the Ponderosa Resort Romantic Comedy Series, and you can nab it right here:

Stiff Suit

books2read.com/u/mg2lpx

Keep reading for a sneak peek from *Stiff Suit* . . .

YOUR EXCLUSIVE SNEAK PEEK AT STIFF SUIT

JAMES

ROLOGUE

Dear diary,

I'm in hell.

There's simply no other way to describe the fact that I'm sitting at a conference table scribbling like a pre-teen girl in a leather-bound journal which I swear to God my sister would have covered with flowery stickers if I hadn't wrenched the damn thing from her hands.

We're supposed to be writing our feelings, which is asinine.

Fine.

What I'm feeling right now is irritated that Bree wrangled us into this conference room under the pretense of reviewing the resort's Q4 marketing plan. Instead, my freshly pregnant sister blindsided us with a family therapy session complete with a bespectacled shrink named—I kid you not—Dr. Hooter. The esteemed doctor is watching over us like a constipated head-mistress who found a frog in her bed.

Mark's in the corner gripping his pencil in a fist, possibly contemplating stabbing himself in the eye to get out of this. Sean's scribbling like mad, but it's probably a to-do list for his wedding in a few days. Even Jonathan's here, visiting between humanitarian missions and probably regretting this stop considerably right now. He's been here just a handful of times since our father's funeral, and I suspect he'll run like hell once this is over.

Secrets.

Headmistress Hooter just said that word.

She said several other words, too, but I tuned her out because I'm busy thinking about how I need to get back to my office and run the TRT numbers for this week.

Fine, she has a point. The Bracelyn family has a history of bottling up our biggest secrets and shaking the Dom Perignon bottle until it explodes all over our interpersonal relationships. Sean, Bree, Mark...everyone's done it, which is precisely why Bree wrangled us in here today.

Reading my mind—God forbid—my sister looks up from her journal and smiles. Then she waves her pen like a wand, urging me to keep writing. I'm considering walking out to get coffee. Brazil, maybe.

Then Bree shifts uncomfortably, resting a hand on the rounded bump that's incubating my niece or nephew, and something softens inside me.

Goddam it, I love my family.

Fine. Dr. Hooter thinks we have secrets?

She doesn't know the half of it.

Has no idea what it's like to be the oldest in a family sired by a patriarch who changed wives with the frequency his fellow billionaires swap sports cars. Cort Bracelyn never liked cars. He liked women, and he liked spreading his DNA around the far reaches of the Earth. That's why we're all here.

Maybe the Bracelyn spawn weren't raised with much connection to each other, but we've taken our late father's vanity ranch and turned it into the top luxury resort in the Pacific Northwest, thank you very much.

I miss the asshole sometimes. Our father, I mean.

How's that for a secret?

Cort Bracelyn—a man whose disinterest in raising children was superseded only by his interest in producing them—still leaves me wishing I could pick up the phone and call him. He always had the best stock tips, and the bastard could make me laugh.

I glance up again, and Jonathan's watching me. Christ, it blows me away sometimes how much he looks like our father. Same build, same cleft chin, same green eyes. He glances at Headmistress Hooter, sees her back is turned, flips me the bird and grins.

Nice. I dip my chin to my necktie, hoping no one sees me smirking. There, that's a secret, right?

But it's nothing like the ones I've kept for our father. The secrets Cort Bracelyn entrusted to his firstborn are hardly fodder for a journal tucked under my pillow each night.

Some secrets you don't put in writing.

Some secrets you share with no one.

Some secrets you swear on all that's holy you will take to your goddamned grave.

***

DON'T MISS OUT!

Want access to exclusive excerpts, behind-the-scenes stories about my books, cover reveals, and prize giveaways? Not only will you get all that by subscribing to my newsletter, but I'll even throw you a **FREE** short story featuring a swoon-worthy marriage proposal for Sean and Amber from *Chef Sugarlips.*

Get it right here.

http://tawnafenske.com/subscribe/

ACKNOWLEDGMENTS

Thank you first and foremost to the readers who've fallen in love with this series, and who make writing it the most fun I've had with my clothes on.

Big gooey gobs of thanks to Fenske's Frisky Posse for all the behind-the-scenes help naming characters, choosing cover art, and offering virtual butt pats. Thanks especially to Leila Schweiss for naming Libby.

For the moral support and early reads, I issue a zillion wheelbarrow loads of gratitude to Linda Grimes and Kait Nolan (both of whom write amazing books, so you should all go out and grab them now).

Thank you to Meah Meow for keeping my shit together in all the ways that matter.

I'm super grateful to Susan Bischoff and Lauralynn Elliott of The Forge for all your hard work massaging my words, and to Lori Jackson Design for the fantastic teaser graphics, banners, and bookmarks.

Much love and gratitude to my family, Aaron "Russ" Fenske and Carlie Fenske, and Paxton, along with and Dixie and David Fenske for always being there. Thanks also to Cedar and Violet for inspiring little bits of Libby, along with my certainty that family needs no matching DNA.

And thank you to my cover designer, web guru, newsletter manager, and bedwarmer, who happens to be all one guy, and also happens to be the love of my life. Craig Zagurski, you're the best thing that ever happened to me. Love you, babe.

ABOUT THE AUTHOR

When Tawna Fenske finished her English lit degree at 22, she celebrated by filling a giant trash bag full of romance novels and dragging it everywhere until she'd read them all. Now she's a RITA Award finalist, USA Today bestselling author who writes humorous fiction, risqué romance, and heartwarming love stories with a quirky twist. Publishers Weekly has praised Tawna's offbeat romances with multiple starred reviews and noted, "There's something wonderfully relaxing about being immersed in a story filled with over-the-top characters in undeniably relatable situations. Heartache and humor go hand in hand."

Tawna lives in Bend, Oregon, with her husband, step-kids, and a menagerie of ill-behaved pets. She loves hiking, snowshoeing, standup paddleboarding, and inventing excuses to sip wine on her back porch. She can peel a banana with her toes and loses an average of twenty pairs of eyeglasses per year. To find out more about Tawna and her books, visit www.tawnafenske.com.

ALSO BY TAWNA FENSKE

The Ponderosa Resort Romantic Comedy Series

Studmuffin Santa

Chef Sugarlips

Sergeant Sexypants

Hottie Lumberjack

Stiff Suit

Mancandy Crush (novella)

Captain Dreamboat

Snowbound Squeeze (novella)

Dr. Hot Stuff (coming soon!)

The Juniper Ridge Romantic Comedy Series

Show Time (coming soon!)

Standalone Romantic Comedies

The Two-Date Rule

At the Heart of It

This Time Around

Now That It's You

Let it Breathe

About That Fling

Frisky Business

Believe It or Not

Making Waves

The Front and Center Series

Marine for Hire

Fiancée for Hire

Best Man for Hire

Protector for Hire

The First Impressions Series

The Fix Up

The Hang Up

The Hook Up

The List Series

The List

The Test

The Last

Standalone novellas and other wacky stuff

Going Up (novella)

Eat, Play, Lust (novella)